TRANSFORMED
by LOVE

TRANSFORMED
by LOVE

CHRISTINE GINSBURY

XULON ELITE

Xulon Press Elite
2301 Lucien Way #415
Maitland, FL 32751
407.339.4217
www.xulonpress.com

Unless otherwise indicated, Scripture quotations taken from the Holy Bible, New Living Translation (NLT). Copyright ©1996, 2004, 2007 by Tyndale House Foundation. Used by permission of Tyndale House Publishers, Inc.

Paperback ISBN-13: 978-1-66286-088-1
Ebook ISBN-13: 978-1-66286-089-8

Table of Contents

Introduction

Dear Reader,

The stories you are about to read are based on nine miracles performed by Jesus as recorded in the Gospels. I have long been curious about the people involved in these miracles—what their lives were like before they met Jesus and how their encounters with him changed them.

This is a work of historical fiction, although the people in each story lived during the time of Christ and met him. I have woven the true stories of their encounters with him into a narrative around each person, imagining how their lifestyles, disabilities, or illnesses affected them before they experienced the miracles and how their lives changed afterwards. In some cases where a name is not given to one of the people in the Biblical account, I have created a name for them. I have given the Gospel references at the end of each story so that you can read the original stories from the Bible.

In writing these stories I have tried to describe as accurately as possible what life was like in the land of Israel in the first century A.D. when Jesus walked the earth so the reader can get as true a picture as possible of each character's lifestyle.

My hope is that as you read these stories you will realise how the love of God completely transforms lives.

At the end I have added a sketch of the children who were brought to Jesus, trying to keep as closely as possible to the original text in the Gospels, as well as two poems that were inspired by my personal meditation on the supreme sacrifice of Jesus Christ, both in his attitude of servanthood and his willingness to share in our suffering.

Chapter One

THE TOUCH

THE SUN SPRINKLED silver on the still blue-grey waters of the Sea of Galilee. On the far side, the hills were still shrouded in mist. After the squall of the previous night, the water rested like an innocent sleeping child.

Little fishing boats were bobbing happily in the middle of the sea as brawny, bare-chested fishermen, weary from a night's fishing, heaved their nets into their vessels and headed back toward the shore.

Overhead, sea birds circled, flapping their wings and crying loudly in anticipation of salvaging something from the catch.

Men were busy on the beach, loading the silvery grey catch already brought in into barrels standing nearby. Some were loading their fishing tackle into dilapidated shacks.

One tanned, barefooted man sat on the beach and mended his frayed net with an awl. Another was weaving new twine into a torn sail.

Dragging his feet sluggishly, a bearded man dressed in torn sackcloth struggled painfully down the hillside overlooking the sea.

About halfway down he reached the rock he habitually visited, he flung himself onto the ground and waited. Several minutes later he heard his mother's voice calling his name.

"Caleb, Caleb my son." A black-robed figure appeared round the bend of the hill and lowered her weary body carefully and wearily, onto a flat rock.

"I've... brought you... some bread and fish." She spoke breathlessly as she pulled out the food folded in her head scarf and placed it on the ground, with a skin of water.

"How are you today?"

Everything within him longed to run toward his mother and hug her. It pained him that he would probably never be able to fulfil that wish. He heaved a sigh and in the low, guttural voice he had now become used to, lied, "I'm fine, Mother. The people at the colony are so kind. They look after me well."

The woman found it hard to look at her son's face, which was swathed in filthy bandages that failed to disguise the hole where his nose should have been and the red and white blotches and lumps on his cheeks.

She began to talk compulsively, giving him the latest news about his uncle, aunt, and cousins. Although she had given him the news of his relatives many times, Caleb listened patiently, happy to drink in the sight of his beloved mother, hoping that time would stand still forever. But eventually, the woman heaved her body resignedly off the rock and, with tears in her eyes, blew a kiss to her son and began to make her way back along the path she had followed.

Caleb waited till she had disappeared round the corner of the hill. The continuous wailing of the seabirds jarred his nerves as he crawled with difficulty toward the food his mother had left on the ground, his stubby fingers digging into the mud of the hillside.

His need for food was so urgent that he couldn't resist cramming one of the bread loaves hungrily into his misshapen mouth. The remaining provision he stuffed into a cloth bag, which he slung round his shoulder before making his way laboriously up the hill.

He was aware of the constant rhythm of the waves sloshing on the pebbles of the shore as he ascended the steep incline. Some people were walking by, so he lifted the heavy bell he carried. Its metallic tone rang out, sounding its threatening warning as the leper reluctantly cried out the words he hated with every fibre of his being, "Unclean! Unclean!"

One of the men spat in his direction and commented to his companion, "What a filthy, disgusting creature." But Simon had become immune to such comments and turned away as he heard the words, refusing to let them hurt him.

He shuffled his way slowly and wearily to the edge of Capernaum. The elders, ready to hear any disputes that were brought to them, sat by the entrance to the town but recoiled at his approach. Passers-by glared at him unpleasantly and moved fearfully away, muttering low-pitched insults as he walked on his way back to the leper colony, which had been his home for the past twenty years.

Chapter Two

THE FOLLOWING DAY, just as the sun was venturing cautiously above the horizon, sprinkling the waters below with silvery light, the man laboured down the hill to return to the place of rendezvous with his mother and waited expectantly for her arrival. Fifteen minutes went by, then thirty. He couldn't understand what was delaying her. She was never late. He settled resignedly onto a low rock and continued to wait.

He stared at the patches of yellow flowers that adorned the hillside until his mind drifted into the past as he struggled with the memory of how his leprosy had been discovered. In his imagination he saw the young fifteen-year-old rising to his feet in the early morning as a faint light penetrated the narrow slits in the wall of his house, casting ominous shadows into the room.

A low mooing sound from the side of the house told him he had awakened the animals as he tiptoed quietly so as not to disturb his widowed mother still sleeping peacefully on her mat. He stepped into the main body of the room and dragged a pitcher from one corner, then lifted it and poured some water into a clay wash bowl. Gingerly he carried the bowl to the courtyard outside.

He peeled his tunic over his head and bent over the bowl to wash his face. He heard the sound of voices as neighbours were starting to make their way to work, and they called out friendly greetings to the young man. Suddenly one man stopped and exclaimed, "What is that?" The young boy turned abruptly at the sound.

"Brother, you have peculiar white patches on your back. I don't like the look of them."

"W-What do you mean?" spluttered the puzzled boy. Fear seized him.

Some of the other men had also stopped and were staring with horror at Caleb's back.

"It looks like leprosy; those spots look very much like leprosy," spluttered another man.

"No! You have to be wrong," shouted Caleb.

"I don't see it anywhere," but staring down at his exposed arm, he spotted a round red bump he hadn't noticed before.

He rushed into his house and flung on a fresh tunic to cover the offending marks. Disturbed by the noise, his mother stirred and sat up on her mat. "What is going on?" she asked.

Caleb hastened to reassure her that all was well, but a crowd had begun to form in the doorway. They were yelling indignantly and pointing at the young boy. "He's got leprosy! Get him out of here! We don't want to catch it!"

"No, you're wrong! You must be wrong!" By now Caleb was panicking. "They'll go away. I know they'll go away," he protested in desperation.

"What will go away?" asked his mother, who had now risen and was putting a robe over the top of her night tunic, embarrassed to see the neighbours watching her.

"Look at his back Martha! Look at his back!" yelled one of the people in the crowd. "We don't want no leper in this neighbourhood!"

The woman warily lifted the boy's tunic and gave an anguished cry as she discovered the white blotches on her son's skin.

"You see! He's got leprosy! We told you!" screamed a woman. "He's got to go!"

Mother and son stared at each other in silent dismay. There were tears in the boy's eyes. They both knew what this meant. Leprosy was regarded as a filthy contagious disease, and anyone with the complaint would be banished from society until they either recovered or died. Everyone knew the latter was the fate of most.

"Leave us alone!" cried the distraught woman. Get out of our house!" We will go to the priest! He will tell us if it is leprosy, not you!" shouted the woman angrily, but in her heart, she feared the worst.

Mumbling, the neighbours drifted away, leaving the woman and her son to face their predicament. The woman looked despairingly at her son.

"We will go now and get you checked by the priest. It is the law. We must obey. I'm sure he will say it is something else that will go away with time."

Sadly, the two left the house and made their way to the local synagogue. It was larger than all the surrounding buildings and had a gabled tiled roof, so it stood out from the smaller buildings around it, which had flat clay roofs.

Caleb stared up at the carved image of the pot of manna over the lintel of the door. Wasn't that supposed to remind his people of how God had provided for them when they were in trouble? Surely God would save him now from a fateful future.

Mother and son approached and slowly ascended the broad steps toward the front door.

The priest was standing behind the bema in the centre of the building, studying the Scriptures. When he heard the loud banging on the door, he heaved an irritated sigh. He rolled up the scroll, lifted it carefully, and replaced it in one of the clay jars used to preserve the sacred scrolls before making his way to the front door.

He instantly recognised the woman and boy standing at the top of the steps and greeted them in a friendly fashion. "Shalom, Martha and Caleb. How can I help you today?"

"Greetings, Joshua, we need you to examine some spots on my son's back. I'm sure it's nothing, but I know we are required by the Law to present to you for examination," Martha hastily explained. "We need to put the neighbours' minds at rest that it's nothing to worry about."

The young priest frowned. "I will have to do the examination outside just in case..." he began. "You can sit on a seat inside." He turned to Martha. "If it is what you fear," he said, "Caleb will not be allowed to enter the synagogue."

Joshua turned to the young boy. "Come with me," he said.

Caleb reluctantly followed.

Taking the boy round the side of the building, Joshua asked him to remove his tunic. With a heavy heart the boy slowly drew his clothing over his head and looked pleadingly at the priest, who now stared at the white spots on the boy's back.

"Do you have any other marks?" he asked.

Caleb held out his right arm to reveal the deep red bump just above his wrist and held his breath. After a few seconds the priest raised his head slowly and, with sad eyes, spoke the dreaded words.

"I'm afraid this is definitely leprosy. You know the Law. You mustn't associate with anyone healthy. You will have to live outside the town with other lepers. If you come into Capernaum and see some people, you must ring a bell and declare yourself 'unclean.' Wait here." He disappeared into the building and came back carrying a tunic of sackcloth.

"You must wear this." He held out the offending article.

Caleb stared at the garment in horror.

"I can't wear my own clothes?" he stammered.

The priest shook his head. "It is prescribed. Now I will tell your mother that she must go. You will not be able to come close to her again."

But I need to say farewell at least..." the boy started to say but reeled with shock as Joshua shook his head.

"No, it is forbidden."

Tears welled up in the boy's eyes. "At least let me wave goodbye to her."

Joshua brought Martha outside and explained to her that it was indeed leprosy and she could not come near her son again. She gave a stifled sob and stared at the priest with an anguished expression. But she knew it was pointless to argue. She knew the Law.

"Can't I see him again?" she sobbed.

"You can bring him food each day, but you must stand six feet from him or even further if the wind is blowing."

"Son, I will bring you food each day, but where shall we meet?"

The young boy took some time to absorb all that had been said, so there was a long pause before he replied. Then with an effort, he muttered in a strangled tone, "Can we meet on the hillside above where I used to fish by the sea of Galilee at five every morning?"

His mother moved toward him, yearning to hug him, but the priest held her back.

"You can ask a neighbour to bring his bed back here. I will wait with him till you return."

She nodded through her tears and turned to go. Caleb called after her. "Who will look after you now? What will you do without me to work?"

His mother hesitated, then, looking down at the ground, mumbled, "Don't worry about me. I'm sure my sister and her husband will take care of me."

The two stared at each other for some seconds. Reluctantly Martha turned and walked away.

Whilst they waited, the priest explained to Caleb where the leper colony was on the outskirts of town.

"Will I ever recover?" he asked the priest, hopefully.

Joshua shook his head pityingly "It's rare, but if you do, you must come straight back to me again so I can declare you clean."

Chapter Three

CALEB SHOOK HIMSELF out of his melancholy reverie and looked up. The sun had climbed higher in the sky,
and he estimated he had been daydreaming for at least an
hour, but there was still no sign of his mother. The voices of
the fishermen drifted up toward him, reminding him of how
he had earned his living in his youth before the leprosy had
stolen his life away.

Now he was worried. His mother had always been very
punctual, and he couldn't think of any reason why she should
be so delayed. He started to fear the worst, but he agonised
over the thought that he would not be welcome to go to his
house to find out what had happened to her.

Sadly, he ascended the hillside and made his way back to
the colony. He thought back to the day he had arrived there
for the first time. He had not been prepared for the sight that
greeted his eyes. Grotesque figures with missing toes and fingers shuffled painfully to and fro in what seemed like a night-
mare vision. Toothless, deformed faces stared blankly at him.
He watched as some men and women stumbled around with
sightless eyes, feeling their way.

Caleb stood for some time, gaping in horror, the realisation slowly dawning on him that what he was viewing was his own future. Tears filled his eyes and a profound sense of hopelessness descended upon him.

Suddenly he felt a tap on his shoulder. Turning, he looked into the red blotched face of a man he judged to be about thirty years old. "Hello," said the man, his voice deep and guttural. "Have you got it? Have they sent you packing? I was about your age when I first came here. I remember how it felt. Most of the lepers here live in caves or tents. Have you brought a tent?"

The young boy hastily rubbed the tears from his eyes and shook his head.

"Then you can share our cave. There are five more of us, but I guess we can make room for one more."

Caleb gave a weak smile and managed a "Thank you."

"My name is Joseph," said the friendly man. What is yours?"

"Caleb." He found he could barely speak as the words seemed reluctant to leave his throat.

"Come with me," Joseph said. "I'll show you the cave"

Caleb followed him into the cave in a zombie-like daze. He was aware of a sickly putrid smell as he walked through the entrance, and he instinctively raised his arm to cover his nose. Once his eyes had become accustomed to the dim light, he saw four other lepers sitting dejectedly on the cold stone floor. They barely looked up as he approached.

Joseph explained that his new friend had just arrived at the colony. "We can make room for one more, can't we?" he asked. A faint shrug of shoulders suggested to Caleb that he was accepted.

Joseph shuffled to the back of the narrow cave, which seemed not more than ten feet in length, and returned with some objects. "Here, you will need this," he suggested, handing Caleb a bell tied to a rope. "You will have to ring this if you encounter any people in the town."

The young boy knew what that was for. He had often passed by ragged lepers at a distance of about six feet, as required by the Law, and observed them ringing a bell and shouting "Unclean! Unclean!" He remembered the mixture of fear and repulsion he had felt at the sight of them. Now it was to be his turn. He almost felt ashamed of his reaction as he realised he would now be the victim of such responses.

Joseph handed him a bowl.

"Here, this is your begging bowl. These belonged to Simeon. He died last week."

Caleb felt he should respond with compassion and muttered, "I'm sorry to hear that."

"No, don't be. We all envy him. At least he doesn't have to suffer anymore.

It took Caleb a few days to find the words to speak at any length to his new companions in suffering. Gradually they began to open up about their life stories and feelings. The one loss that seemed to be the greatest for all of them was that they could no longer be touched and hugged by their loved ones. They no longer felt accepted or valued. Even the companionship of other lepers didn't make up for such great needs.

Day after day Caleb returned to the meeting place, but there was no sign of his mother. Without her willingness to bring him food, he would have to rely on begging, and he knew from the other lepers in the colony, who had no relatives to help them, that very little food was supplied.

On the fifth day, as he was about to give up, he hung his head in despair and cried, "Oh God. What am I to do? Why have you brought me to this place? I wish I were dead."

Just then he heard the rumbling of new voices. The sound grew closer, and looking up, he saw an imposing figure of medium height with a beard and dark hair falling to his shoulders. The man had a look of quiet confidence about him. He was followed by a large crowd of men, women, and children. Fearing that his presence might be discovered, the man slunk behind a tall rock and peered round inquisitively at the assembled company.

The rabbi began to address the crowd in a voice that sounded gentle yet authoritative. He began telling stories as his audience listened with rapt attention. Caleb couldn't help being enthralled by the voice, and he listened with a growing sense of awe.

This teacher didn't seem like all the others. Caleb remembered how, on one occasion, he had overheard a rabbi complaining that he wouldn't even buy a fish in a street where a leper had been. And on another, a rabbi had picked up rocks to throw at him. He had just managed to run away before they struck him.

But this man talked about blessing the poor and needy, about loving your enemy and doing good to those who hurt you. He also talked of a Kingdom he said was not of this world. He had a godlike quality about him, and Caleb felt a growing respect for him that kept him attached to the rock like a magnet.

When the man finished speaking, people began crying out to him, calling him "Jesus." They were bringing the sick and disabled to him, and Caleb watched in amazement as this man called Jesus calmly spoke words of healing over them. One after another he witnessed limbs growing back, lame people throwing away their sticks and walking, blind men shouting they could see, and others proclaiming their deafness had gone.

A surge of hope rose in Caleb's heart like a heavy stone long buried in the sea, now rising to the surface.

He waited until all the crowd had drifted away, their voices floating fainter and fainter on the air. The rabbi was left with a group of men Caleb judged to be his close friends. He too turned to go, and Caleb realised he had to make a move. Otherwise it might be too late and he might never see this man again.

He shuffled from behind the rock where he was hiding and, flinging himself down, prostrated himself on the dry, dusty mud of the hillside path. His heart was beating fast. He hardly dared hope for a response. Suppose the teacher walked on without paying him any attention, or worse still, responded with a derisory look. Well, what did he have to lose? He was like a dead man anyway.

But something urged him on. He had watched this man heal all sorts of conditions. All he had to do was speak some words and perhaps... just perhaps the leprosy would go. He summoned every bit of energy he had and in a deep, husky, pleading voice cried out, "Lord, if you are willing, you can heal me and make me clean." He held his breath.

The man turned and began walking toward him. Caleb was surprised. Didn't he realise the risk he was taking, coming so near? But the teacher was within inches of him and, stretching out his arms, took Caleb by the shoulders and drew him close. Then he placed his right hand onto the greasy tangled hair of his head.

Something heavy and strangled, a long-forgotten hunger, broke inside the leper, something that had lain dormant for years. A piteous cry came from deep in his chest. All he could think was, *He touched me! He touched me!*

Lifting his head, he looked into the most beautiful eyes of pure compassion and love, and in that instant, Caleb felt accepted and valued. Something in him knew he was looking into the face of God. All Jesus said was, "I am willing. Be healed."

Instantly Caleb felt as if a sudden current of electricity flowed into his body, starting at his feet and igniting his legs, torso, and arms till it reached his head that buzzed as with fire. Looking down at his feet he watched in wonder as toes grew back, then fingers. The unsightly red welts and bumps on his legs and arms disappeared. He reached his hands to his face and above the grizzled beard he felt soft, flat skin and a perfectly formed nose. Tears of joy began flowing down Caleb's face.

Then an expression of sternness appeared in Jesus' eyes, yet as he spoke the healed man knew he was speaking with concern for him. "Don't tell anyone about this. Just go to the priest and let him examine you. Take along the offering required in the Law of Moses for those who have been healed of leprosy. This will be a public testimony that you have been cleansed."

Jesus turned to go, and Caleb cried after him, "Thank you, thank you...."

He found himself skipping with joy as he made his way half running, half tumbling up the hillside. Despite the rabbi's warning, he couldn't help but call out excitedly, "I'm healed! I'm healed! Jesus did it!"

People stopped and stared at him in disbelief. Caleb was shocked to hear himself speak. His low, guttural voice had been replaced by a normal tone.

His inclination was to make his way through the town to his house to find out what had happened to his mother, but first he had to obey the command to show himself to a priest. Reluctantly he turned in the direction of the synagogue, hoping he would meet the priest, Joshua, who had examined him all those years ago.

Chapter Four

WHEN CALEB ARRIVED at the synagogue, a rabbi was just finishing his teaching to a group of people. He dismissed them and they began to file out through the front entrance. They stared curiously at the dishevelled figure. Out of habit, Caleb dodged aside to put space between himself and the crowd. When they had all gone, he climbed the steps and nervously hesitated at the door.

The rabbi lifted the handle of the scroll from the groove of the carved stone block on which it was sitting and carefully rolled it up. Lifting it, he carried it lovingly and reverently to the back of the synagogue, where he placed it in a clay jar behind a pillar. Turning, he saw a dirty figure with long greasy hair, dressed in sackcloth and hovering at the doorway.

Oh no, he thought. *What does this fellow want? Money, no doubt.*

"I was hoping to see the priest, Joshua," Caleb said.

The rabbi looked at the scruffy figure with distrust. "He will be here in about half an hour. What did you want to see him about?"

Caleb wondered if he should tell this priest his story, but he decided to say nothing. He simply explained that he needed Joshua's help. "I'll come back later," he said, although he felt disappointed that he had to wait.

Caleb hid out of sight until the rabbi left the synagogue. He waited impatiently.

Sometime later Joshua appeared. He looked so much older and walked slowly toward the doors of the building.

Caleb plucked up the courage to move toward the priest. "Joshua," he said.

The priest turned to confront the scruffy individual approaching him.

"Do I know you?" He peered at Caleb's face.

"I'm Caleb. You diagnosed me with leprosy twenty years ago, but a rabbi called Jesus healed me, and look at me! I am completely clean!" he blurted out enthusiastically.

The old priest started, "How... how... Yes... yes... I do remember you... but it's not possible...."

"Jesus... Jesus the rabbi healed me. He actually touched me, Joshua.... he touched me. He wasn't worried about catching the leprosy. Who is he, Joshua? I have never met anyone like him. He had such love and compassion in his eyes. I have never felt so accepted by anyone....and look at me.... My fingers and toes have grown back and there is not a mark on me." He flung out his arms in proof. He told me to come and see you. You can declare me clean and then I can return home."

"Not so fast" the priest protested. "It isn't as simple as that." He moved closer to Caleb and peered into his face: "I remember you now. I certainly didn't expect to see you again... and looking so normal"

He took Caleb aside and began to examine his body.

"Tell me more about this Jesus you speak of. I think I know who you mean. I was present when a rabbi they referred to as Jesus preached in this very synagogue. I must admit he spoke with a kind of authority I have never observed before. The people were very impressed by him. Apparently, they follow him everywhere, and the word is he has performed many miracles.

He glanced over his shoulder furtively and lowered his voice.

"I have tried to find out more about him, but I have to be careful because the Pharisees and scribes don't like him. They say he blasphemes God. I am very surprised that he told you to come and see me. I heard that he doesn't obey the whole Law. He heals on the Sabbath and mixes with tax collectors and sinners."

"Well, who do you think he is? I can't believe he blasphemes. I have never seen such God-like eyes before. And I'm convinced he was thinking of my good when he told me to come to you. He must have known no one would accept me back into society until I had a certificate of health," Caleb protested vehemently.

"I don't know, but it is more than my job is worth to speak well of him publicly. But if you do find out any more about him, come and tell me."

"I will" said Caleb, "but can I have the certificate? I need to get home. I haven't seen my mother for days and I fear she is ill."

Joshua sighed, "Come with me"

He opened the door of the synagogue again and Caleb followed him down the aisle, past the stone pillars to the centre. Joshua took out a large scroll from one of the clay jars and placed it carefully on the stone block. He wedged the handles of the scroll in the grooves of the stone frame.

"This is the scroll of Leviticus." He pointed at the writing as he unfurled the scroll to about halfway through.

"See, here it tells you what you have to do before you can return to your friends and family."

Sighing deeply, Caleb peered at the Hebrew writing on the scroll. He knew what it said. Before his father died, he had taught him the writings of the Torah well. But as he read, the scroll reminded him of what he would have to do as the Rabbi Jesus had said: make an offering of a lamb or two live birds, some flour, and some oil.

"But," he began, "do I have to go all the way to Jerusalem to make these offerings at the temple? And how am I to get these things, not to mention the hyssop and cedar wood, without any money?" Despair had filled his heart once again. All he wanted to do was get to his home and be reunited with his mother.

The priest nodded grimly. "You will not be accepted back into society until you do this." He was touched by Caleb's dejected expression and added, "But I will lend you the money. You can buy the items for the offering when you get to the temple. I will go and see your mother and tell her what has happened. If she is sick, maybe the news of your recovery will revive her.

Now you need to wash and put on some clean clothes. He led Caleb outside to the mikveh. I will go to your mother and find out how she is. I will tell her you will return when you have made the required sacrifice. Take this robe and I will bring you back some of your clothes and sandals." He handed Caleb a long tunic.

The young man's eyes clouded with tears at the kindness of the priest.

"Tell my mother I will come to her as soon as I return from Jerusalem."

The priest urged Caleb to be quick because he knew a group of people would be coming to see a rabbi to settle a dispute later that day, and he was feeling a little guilty that he had let the young man into the vicinity of the synagogue as he had not yet been declared clean.

Chapter Five

CALEB WAS GLAD to wash himself and looked proudly at his new body—completely free of sores. He put on the priest's robe, which came short of his ankles and looked a bit ridiculous, but he was so grateful for the fresh garment that he did not feel entitled to complain.

As he was walking back to the synagogue, he heard voices and had just enough time to dodge round the corner of the building before a group of people appeared.

It was hard to wait for the priest to return, and as he was alone with his thoughts, Caleb's anxiety about his mother plagued him. Suppose she was dead. Suppose she was ill but died before he could see her. He lifted his hands upward and said a prayer, asking God to keep his mother safe till he returned.

It was some hours before Joshua came back.

"Tell me. How is my mother?" Caleb urged.

The priest looked earnestly into the man's eyes.

"Martha is very sick. She has not been able to leave her bed for days. But your aunt is looking after her. When I told her your story it seemed to revive her somewhat. Martha is a good woman. She knows the Law and understands that, as hard as it is, she cannot see you until you have made your offering."

He handed a tunic, a sleeveless cloak, and sandals to Caleb and urged him to leave as soon as possible. Handing him a cloth purse of money, he said, "This will be enough to obtain what you need for the offering and to buy some food for the journey."

Gratefully Caleb took the money, and after exchanging the robe for the new garments, he left the synagogue and headed for Jerusalem.

Ten days later Caleb arrived back in Capernaum, lovingly clutching his certificate of cleansing. His one ambition was to get to his home and see his beloved mother. All the way back he had prayed fervently that she would not die till he could be with her.

He began to run through the tangle of streets. Potter Street was filled with colourful wares as the craftsmen sat outside their shops and displayed their pots. On Carpenter Street, tables and chairs were piled high for display. As Caleb made his way through the streets, he repeatedly bumped into men with handcarts, laden donkeys, and carrying heavy loads. People stared at this anxious man careering through their streets, quite oblivious to the noise and bustle of busy people and children shouting with glee as they played. He did not stop to greet anyone but pursued his course with a determination they could not understand.

Eventually Caleb arrived at his house. He stopped and paused for a moment to get his breath. The sun shining on the stones made the home seem alive. He looked up at the flat roof where he saw the washing drying in the sun and remembered how he had watched his mother hang out the clothes on many occasions.

He noticed children playing noisily in the dust below, throwing quoits and chasing each other, and thought back to his early childhood when he had played those same games.

Home... Home.... he thought—the place he never thought he would see again. Tears welled up in his eyes.

Whoever you are, Jesus, he reflected, *I will never be able to thank you enough.*

He walked into the courtyard where it had all begun, painfully remembering the voices of the crowd yelling at him to leave. But now the only sounds that intruded on his thoughts were those of "mooing" and "baaing" as he stroked the nose of a goat that had approached him and began nudging him.

He pushed open the door to the house and stood for a moment, letting his eyes adjust to the dimness of the room, lit by two solitary oil lamps.

Then he turned to the right to the raised platform of the room. It was then he saw the figures of two women, one lying down and one at her side, tending her. He rushed up the steps and flung himself down beside the prostrate figure, crying, "Mother, Mother. I'm home. I'm healed."

The other woman got up and moved to the other side of the room.

The young man's words tumbled out of him as he said, "Did the priest tell you? I wanted so much to come home ten days ago, but I couldn't till I got this."

He reached into his tunic and pulled out the parchment scroll that gave him his freedom and waved it triumphantly in the air.

His mother opened her eyes and light filled them with joy. She spoke weakly.

"I know, my son. God has graciously kept me for this moment."

Caleb lovingly slid his arm underneath his mother's head and shoulders and gently raised her up and held her. He began to tell her how he had met with the rabbi, Jesus, how he had touched him, and how he was instantly healed.

"Now I can go to my fathers in peace," said his mother faintly.

"No, no. You are going to get better. I will look after you. You cannot leave me now. I have returned." Caleb could not receive his mother's words.

"My time has come, son. But I thank the Lord for preserving me for this moment. I can go in peace now, to my fathers."

She took a few moments to recover her breath. Then, looking directly at Caleb she said, "I have heard of this Jesus. Some say he is the coming Messiah. You must find him and follow him, my son. He has healed you for a purpose."

Caleb's heart ached. He wanted to scream. "No, no mother. You can't leave me now." But she closed her eyes and sank back into her son's arms. Her body went limp, and he rocked her back and forth for some time till her body went cold and stiff.

Sobbing, Caleb lowered his mother's frame down onto the mat; got up; and, realising his aunt had gone to the court-yard to leave mother and son alone, went to fetch her.

As he stepped outside, oblivious to the mingled sounds of the animals and children, his mother's last words came back to him as if she was speaking with urgency inside his head. *You must find him and follow him. He has healed you for a purpose.*

In that instant, Caleb knew that is just what he had to do.

But that is a story for another day.

Bible References: Matthew 8:1-4; Mark 1: 40 – 45; Luke 5:12-16

Innovation

The Friend's Story

JOEL HAD KNOWN Nathaniel for years. They played together as boys and Nathaniel used to outstrip his companions in running races.

But that all ended after his illness, three years previously when he was paralysed from the waist down. He was not the same person. He once was lively, full of fun, the life and soul of the party, but after his illness he was constantly beset with guilt.

"God is punishing me for my sins," he would moan day and night as he was wracked with guilt. Nothing any of us could say would comfort him.

On the day of the great miracle, Joel and another friend, as was their practice, carried Nathaniel out on his bed and set him under a palm tree so that he could enjoy the sunshine whilst they went off to work.

At mid-morning, Joel was planing down a yoke he was making in his workshop when he heard a loud rumbling that sounded like thunder. It morphed into indistinct voices all talking at once, and he peered out of the doorway to find the reason.

A large crowd, which reminded him of a huge plague of locusts, was surging down the street, everyone talking excitedly. Some were pushing emaciated figures in barrows. The prone, helpless bodies of invalids were being carried on pallets. A crippled old man with pain in his eyes shuffled painfully down the road on crude homemade crutches. A frail, feeble old woman held the hand of a pale and wizened boy. Joel approached a woman carrying a small baby, who was screeching loudly, and asked her the reason for the crowd.

"Haven't you heard?" she shouted above the noise.

"The carpenter, Jesus of Nazareth has come back to Capernaum and is staying at his friend, the fisherman's house. I am taking my baby for healing; we have heard he works miracles."

Joel had heard of this Jesus and was struck by the reference to him as a carpenter, his very own trade. It was rumoured that Caleb, who lived a few streets away, once had leprosy, but a few weeks previously he had been healed by this Jesus.

That gave Joel hope for his friend. Shutting up his workshop, he ran to Nathaniel, and found him sleeping and shook him awake and told him, "I'm going to take you to see another carpenter, Jesus of Nazareth. He's a teacher and they say he heals people. Apparently, he has just returned to Capernaum. He might be able to heal your paralysis."

Nathaniel rubbed his bleary eyes and looked at his friend cynically. "Fat chance I have of being healed," he moaned. "Remember, I am being punished by God for my sins."

Joel felt irritated by his reply.

"At least let us try. You have nothing to lose, have you?" Joel yelled at him.

Nathaniel shrugged his shoulders. "How do you propose to get me there?" he asked.

"Wait here" his friend replied. "I will fetch three more guys and we will carry you on your bed."

"I won't be going anywhere," Nathaniel retorted dryly.

Joel raced off to find his friends, James, Thomas, and Barnabas. They all had workshops nearby. They were all very willing to come and carry Nathaniel to the fisherman's house.

They took the four corners of their friend's mat and heaved it up, Thomas and Joel facing front and James and Barnabas taking up the rear.

"Whoa! You are a ton weight," Thomas complained.

Nathaniel had been quite slim as a young man, but lying still for so long, he had put on quite a lot of weight. Nevertheless, the four young men were determined to get him to Jesus, whatever effort it took.

The sun was very hot, and as they walked, they were sweating profusely and had to stop several times to get their breath.

Simon's house was about a mile from Joel's Street, at about thirty yards from the white stone synagogue and overlooking the Sea of Galilee, but they made it eventually. Joel's heart failed when they saw the mass of people stretching outside the house into the two courtyards.

The house was larger than Joel's, typical of one housing two families, but built of the same coarse black basalt stone. It had several small rooms clustered around the two courtyards, both of which were packed with a throng of people. They were squeezed together, pushing up against each other, some standing on their tiptoes to get a view of the speaker, whose calm, yet commanding voice, filtered out through the eastern doorway. There was a complete hush from the crowd as they seemed to hang on his every word.

The four young men tried to push their way through the throng, repeating, "Excuse me... can you let us through? We must get to Jesus."

But no one budged. Some of them looked angrily round at them, putting a finger to their lips.

"Shush," they reprimanded. "We are trying to hear the rabbi. Don't you think we all want to get close to him?"

Feeling very disheartened, the friends eased the bed to the ground and looked at each other disconsolately.

"That's that then," said Nathaniel, "but thanks for trying anyway, guys."

Joel was not easily defeated, however. An idea was forming in his mind. He had built his own house, including the roof, and knew it was made of crushed limestone rock, earth, and straw supported by crisscrossed tree branches, covered over with baked mud, so he considered it should be possible to break through.

"Quick!" he yelled to his friends. "Lift the bed up the steps to the roof."

"What good will that do?" It was obvious Nathaniel had lost all hope.

"We can make a hole in the roof and let the bed down. If we can get it in front of Jesus, he will surely heal you."

Barnabas, who was the steady one among the friends, looked doubtful.

"I'm not sure the owner of the house will want us to break up his roof," he expostulated.

"Never mind that," replied Joel. "We can worry about that afterwards. Isn't it worth a try?"

They all nodded their heads and, picking up the bed, made for the outdoor steps.

Nathaniel had to grab tightly to the sides of the mat as they hauled him upwards.

"Even if we get through the roof, how are we going to lower him down?" asked practical Barnabas.

"That's a point" said Joel, feeling somewhat deflated.

"I know," suggested James. "Take off your girdles. We will tie one at each end of the mat."

Whilst James tied the girdles to each end of the wooden poles holding the pallet, the rest of the friends began stamping on the roof. They could hear gasps and murmured comments below, but they persevered until they loosened the mud covering and could see the layer of straw and branches below.

"We need to make it about five feet wide if we are to get the bed through," Barnabas commented. So, they continued stamping until it was wide enough. All eyes were upturned toward the young men, and some people called out unpleasant remarks, but no one was going to stop them now. This was their one hope of getting their friend healed, and they knew, if the rumours were correct, Jesus would heal him.

The teacher was looking up at them, and his face, unlike some of the faces in the crowd, bore an expression of encouragement, even—Joel thought—*admiration.*

They pulled out a few of the tree branches supporting the roof and began to lower Nathaniel on his bed toward Jesus. Straw, dried mud, and ashes were flying everywhere into the protesting crowd. Jesus himself was covered in debris, but he didn't seem to object. He just looked up and smiled reassuringly.

People reached up to help haul the bed downward, and it landed with a jolt right at the rabbi's feet. Joel expected him to reach down, say a few words, and heal his friend. Instead, to his surprise, as the young men peered down through the hole, they heard him say "My son, your sins are forgiven."

Then he turned to some people on his right. It was then Joel noticed the two well-dressed scribes contrasting sharply with the dirty, torn garments of those around them. The expression on their faces showed how shocked and indignant they were. Jesus must have guessed what they were thinking because he spoke to them in a stern voice. Joel couldn't quite catch all the words, but he gathered he was challenging them. Then he turned back to Nathaniel, and, smiling at him, he said, "Stand up, pick up your bed, and walk."

Joel expected Nathaniel to regain his feeling gradually, but to his surprise he leapt to his feet, took hold of his pallet, and proceeded to walk briskly out of the house, shouting praise to God as the crowd made a pathway for him to walk through. They were gabbling words of amazement, praising God, lifting their hands to the heavens.

The friends rushed down the stairs, practically falling over each other to greet Nathaniel, who seemed to be in a kind of daze. They all began talking at once, asking him how it felt and what he thought of what Jesus said to him.

He stopped and looked at his friends with an expression of absolute delight on his face as he said, "He forgave my sins. I can't explain how I felt when he said that. It was as if a massive, heavy load lifted off me, and I sensed a lightness in my spirit. I still feel ecstatic inside. You know the guilt I felt for years? It has all gone...completely gone. And look at me. I can walk—all feeling has returned."

Tears were pouring down his face, and indeed all the friends were blubbering as they hugged him. They walked back home, talking and laughing and giving praise to God. Then Barnabas stopped and, looking somewhat guilty, said, "But what about Simon's roof? We will have to offer to replace it."

"Of course, we will. We will go back tomorrow and offer to mend it, but today we need to celebrate," Joel said.

And that is just what they did.

Simon Peter's Story

EVEN THOUGH JESUS had asked the man he had healed of leprosy, not to tell anyone, the man blurted it to everyone he met. Simon reflected that he could hardly be blamed. Most people would have had trouble keeping that news to themselves after suffering for years. However, the man's revelation made life very awkward for the master, because the multitudes were clamouring to see him. At that time, Jesus didn't want the scribes and Pharisees to get wind of his healings, so he suggested he and his disciples spend a few days alone in the hills till everything calmed down.

Later, Andrew and Simon offered to row him back to Capernaum where their family house was situated. Simon knew his mother-in-law would be especially pleased to see the master because he had healed her when she was dying of a fever.

Simon was looking forward to seeing his wife and children again. When they arrived at the house the three children rushed out to greet them. They were talking at once and showing their father their latest games.

His wife, Rebecca, and her mother started preparing a meal.

No sooner had Jesus and the family finished eating than they heard a familiar sound. A raucous crowd of people were descending on the house.

"Shall I get rid of them?" said Simon's wife. "'I'm sure Jesus is much too tired to see them now."

"No, let them come, Rebecca. They are all needy people. I must teach them and I'm sure they are bringing their sick for healing. After all, that is what I am here for," replied the master.

Simon found his reply somewhat irritating. He had been looking forward to a quiet evening with his family, and he didn't relish the idea of a crowd of noisy, sick people invading his home. But he knew better than to argue with the master.

In they flooded: babies bawling, women crying, children shouting. The noise, not to mention the smell of sweaty bodies and rotting sores, was horrendous. Some were peering through the window openings, straining to get a glimpse of the master. But when Jesus spoke, a great hush fell upon them.

Jesus began by telling stories, as usual, and everyone, including the children, listened intently. Simon was always surprised at how Jesus managed to tell so many different stories.

At one point, Simon heard a disturbance at the eastern courtyard. He guessed someone was trying to push their way in, *but there wasn't much chance of that,* He thought cynically.

The grumbling stopped and all ears were on the master again. It never ceased to amaze Simon how he managed to hold the attention of everyone from the youngest to the oldest.

Suddenly a thunderous sound came from overhead. Simon realised with dismay someone was stamping loudly on his roof. Every head turned upward.

"Oi! What do you think you're doing?" yelled a young man at the front of the mob.

"Clear off!" shouted another, and the rest of the crowd joined in with words that shocked Simon and his family.

Simon looked at his wife in consternation as half his roof came falling down in pieces, mud and straw flying everywhere. People were trying to dodge the debris, while they continued shouting obscenities, till Jesus held up his hand to silence them. Simon was shocked to see him smiling up at the vandals who were destroying his roof.

Then four faces appeared above the hole, and they started lowering a mat with a man lying prone on it. People standing nearby helped bring the mat down to the feet of Jesus.

Everyone held their breath, wondering how the master would respond. He turned to the man on the mat, and to Simon's astonishment, said, "Son, your sins are forgiven. *Well, he* reflected, *I have never heard him address a sick person like that before.*

Jesus turned to look at the people on his right, and it was then Simon noticed the two scribes sitting on his chairs. *How did they manage to sneak in? He* wondered. They always seemed to turn up like bad pennies.

What Jesus said next made Simon frightened for him: "Why do you question this in your hearts?" He always seemed to know what people were thinking. "Is it easier to say to the paralysed man 'your sins are forgiven' or 'stand up, pick up your mat, and walk?"

The two men had gone very red in the face. In fact, Simon smiled inwardly, as he thought one of them was about to explode.

Then Jesus followed his question with these words: "I'll prove to you that the Son of Man has authority to forgive sins."

There was a gasp from the crowd because everyone knows only God can forgive sins. Having said that, the master turned to the paralysed man and, speaking in a more compassionate but authoritative voice, said, "Stand up, pick up your mat and go home."

To Simon's amazement the fellow jumped up, grabbed his bed, slung it over his shoulder, and walked out, as the crowd parted to let him through.

By this time the people had gone hysterical. Some were expressing amazement; some were shouting praise to God. The whole room just erupted.

Brushing the pieces of mud and straw off himself, Jesus held up his hand again, and once more there was total silence.

In a calm voice he began to teach again as if nothing had happened. Simon looked to the right and noticed the scribes had disappeared. In all the excitement they must have slunk off, he imagined, to tell tales to the rulers of the synagogue down the road from his house.

As usual, people started bringing their sick to Jesus, and it was another hour before the master dismissed them and sent them back to their homes.

When the noise of their departure had died down, Simon looked with dismay at the mess on the floor. "That was a bit inconsiderate," He moaned. "Now I will have to repair the roof. It took me two days to build it in the first place. You'd think the men who broke it would have apologised."

Jesus placed a consoling hand on his shoulder and, looking at him sternly, asked, "Simon, what matters more, a hole in your roof, or a man's life given back to him? Those friends today showed so much faith. That is the faith I want you and my other disciples to have if you are to take the kingdom message to the world."

What could he say to that? He felt completely ashamed of his attitude.

Simon's wife and mother-in-law began sweeping up the mess. Fortunately, they had another room in their house besides Andrew's accommodation for his family, so with a bit of shuffling around of family members, no one needed to sleep on the roof as planned.

To their credit, the five men returned the following day and offered to rebuild Simon's roof. The man Jesus had healed expressed his gratitude to the master, and Jesus responded with praise for his friends' faith.

However, Simon couldn't help wondering what message the two scribes had taken back to the synagogue!

The Scribe's Story

THE NEWS THAT the carpenter was back in Capernaum and was staying at the house of the fishermen Simon and Andrew by the lakeside, was reported to the religious leaders in the area. They had instructions to follow him wherever he went, so when Reuben and his fellow scribe, Benjamin, spotted a huge crowd of locals headed in the direction of the house, they realised this was an opportunity to catch him teaching.

There were so many people claiming to be the expected Messiah, and it seemed the people thought this Jesus was the one the Jewish people were expecting. Reuben knew they couldn't allow such strong followings to arise. Any hint of an uprising and the Romans would be down on them like a ton of bricks. This was especially worrying as there was a company of a hundred soldiers, always watching for trouble, stationed in this very town.

By the time Reuben and his companion reached the house, the mob was already crowding into it and overflowing into the courtyards. Of course, the multitudes had to stand back to make way for them to move into the house to get closer to the speaker. They found two chairs to the right and sat down.

The carpenter was holding forth and into his second story when there came a loud banging on the ceiling above. He stopped teaching and the people started looking upward. Suddenly a hole appeared in the roof and four rascally faces peered down at the people. *What impudence,* Reuben thought. *What do they think they are doing?*

Then, a bed on which a man lay supine, appeared and was being lowered to the floor. Reuben fully expected Jesus to reprimand the men on the roof, but when the scribe looked at his face, he was smiling approvingly.

He turned to the prostrate figure and what he said infuriated Reuben: "Son, your sins are forgiven!"

Who on earth did he think he was? Only God could forgive sins, and even then, it must be done in the proper way with the correct ritual of sacrifices in the temple, not in the room of a common fisherman's house. This would be something to report to the authorities. Reuben concluded this man was either mad or the son of the devil.

As Reuben was thinking these thoughts and exchanging looks with his companion, the carpenter turned and looked straight at them. In an insolent voice, he said, "Which is easier to say: 'Your sins are forgiven, or 'Rise, take up your bed, and walk?'"

Well, thought Reuben *anyone can say the words, but that doesn't make them true or right.*

The carpenter followed that statement with these words (The scribe took special note of his exact words so he could give a good account to the authorities): "To prove to you that the Son of Man has power on earth to forgive sins...," and then he turned to the man on the bed and said, "Get up, take your bed, and walk."

There was a gasp from the crowd as the man leapt to his feet and departed. Reuben thought, *They obviously didn't realise it had been a complete setup. The man's recovery was too quick. If he had wanted to make it look more convincing, he could at least have drawn the act out longer.* The idiots were shouting and screaming and going hysterical, so the scribes had a job forcing their way out of the building.

Reuben turned to his fellow scribe, Benjamin, and commented, "That show was obviously prearranged! Jesus must have agreed beforehand with those four louts to make that dramatic entrance so it would draw attention to the so-called miracle. But what impudence... to claim to forgive the man's sins. The man is a blasphemer! We must report this to the synagogue authorities immediately so they can alert the High Priest in Jerusalem as soon as possible."

Benjamin hesitated. "I don't know. There was something about his teaching. He speaks with such authority."

"But," Reuben spluttered, "he had the impertinence to claim to forgive sins! How dare he!"

True," Benjamin replied. "The people were a bit too impressed."

The scribes arrived at the house of Jarius, the ruler of the synagogue, and gave their report. He called on the Hassan and a priest called Nathan, whose houses were near to the synagogue. Nathan was due to travel to Jerusalem the following day and agreed to take the message.

Reuben felt a little annoyed with Jairus because he claimed to have watched the fellow teach and heal and suggested he might be genuine!

He reminded him that they needed to nip in the bud the popularity the man was attracting to himself. Goodness knows what the Roman centurion and his soldiers stationed at the edge of the town would think about the crowds following him.

One thing was certain, Reuben thought: They would have to spy on the fellow as much as they could. It was probable they would send some of the Pharisees and Sadducees to Capernaum to check him out, and Reuben felt quite proud of his day's work. He and Benjamin would be commended for their vigilance. So, the two scribes made sure they found out where the fellow would go next and made plans to follow him.

Biblical references
Matthew 9:1–8; Mark 2:1–12; Luke 5:17–29

A Father's Love

Chapter One

JAIRUS CHECKED THAT all the lamps in the synagogue were extinguished and the clay jars containing the sacred scrolls were closed. Then he moved to the door, locked it for the night, and made his way back to his commodious house, which was near to the synagogue. It had been a tiring day with so many people coming and going, so he was pleased to be retiring for the night.

As he approached his house, his twelve-year-old daughter came running out to greet him. She flung her arms around her father and addressed him excitedly, "Abba, come and see the bread I have made. Mother says it is the best she has tasted."

The man laughed delightedly. This beautiful dark-haired girl, with her sparkling eyes, was the apple of his eye. He had three grown sons, all of whom had left home, but the man and his wife had waited six years for their only daughter.

He remembered the day she was born; she was a little bundle of fun. They had named her Esther after the wonderful woman whose bravery had saved the nation of Israel, and the little girl turned out to be such a happy, intelligent child with great promise.

From the age of two, Jairus had sat Esther on his knee and recited to her stories from the Scriptures, but her favourite, of course, was the story of her namesake. He was proud to see how quickly she had learned the scriptures, and both he and his wife loved to hear her clear, musical voice singing the Psalms.

Now Esther took her father's hand and led him into the house. He laughed at her exuberance as she produced a roll of bread and thrust it enthusiastically toward him. "Taste it," she insisted.

She waited with eager expectation for his response. To tease her, he wrinkled his nose and said, "Ugh! What have you put in this?"

But as her face fell, he laughed heartily and continued, "No, really. It is delicious. You are going to be as good a cook as your mother.

"How is she going to be like her mother?" came the voice of his wife as she walked out from another room to greet her husband.

"You have trained her well," replied Jairus as he kissed his wife.

"I shall be sad when she marries and leaves me. She is such a good little help about the house," remarked Rachel, winking at her daughter.

"Not half as sorry as I am," said her husband, smiling down at his daughter, who was enjoying the compliments. "Don't leave us too soon," he pleaded.

Chapter Two

As RULER OF the Synagogue in Capernaum, it was Jairus' job to arrange services and choose the preacher. He had been told about a new rabbi in the area, a carpenter called Jesus, who apparently came from Nazareth. It was not an area one expected to produce the educated, but people apparently flocked to hear this man, so Jairus was curious to know why he was so popular. He had sent a messenger to find Jesus and invite him to speak the following Sabbath.

The elder was surprised when the man arrived with four friends that he recognised as fishermen, one of them a heavily tanned Galilean who frequently delivered fish to his household.

The prayer leader was standing at the centre of the synagogue, at the bimah, surrounded by the worshippers, who sat on the stone seats on the western and eastern sides of the building. When he had recited the Shema and the Amidah, he stood aside while the attendant handed the Torah scroll, already open at the reading for the day, to Jesus, who had chosen to give the readings himself. Then, passing the scroll back to the attendant, he sat down on the seat to the right, to preach.

Jairus had heard many sermons by rabbis over the years, and most of them he found unenlightening, as they were mainly based on quotes from other rabbis, which they then sought to interpret. So, he wasn't expecting much from this speaker. But as he listened, he became more and more impressed. This man was speaking from the heart, and he seemed to possess a kind of authority in what he said. His words struck a profound note in the elder's consciousness.

When Jesus had finished speaking, he was about to return to his seat next to his friends when something disturbing happened: a bearded man in scruffy, ragged clothes, to the left of the synagogue, stood up and began yelling in an abusive manner: "Let us alone! What have we to do with you, Jesus of Nazareth? Did you come to destroy us? I know who you are, the Holy One of God."

The worshippers looked aghast, and some of them appeared quite frightened. Jairus recognised the man as someone rumoured to be demon-possessed, but the elder was disturbed to hear him refer to Jesus in this way. If anyone else called the teacher "holy one of God," it would be considered blasphemous, so he wondered perhaps if the demon was speaking through the man.

Jairus held his breath, wondering what Jesus would say or do. The elder had watched people conduct exorcisms in the past. Usually they involved long, elaborate, superstitious rituals. One such exorcist he'd witnessed placed a ring, supposedly associated with Solomon, under the nose of the demon-possessed man. As he smelled it, supposedly the ring drew out the demon through the man's nostrils. When the man fell down, the exorcist adjured the demon never to come back into him, reciting incantations he, presumably, had composed.

The exorcist had then placed a cup of water a little way off and commanded the demon, as it went out of the man, to overturn it and convince the bystanders that it had indeed left him.

Jairus groaned within himself, wondering if Jesus would give such a performance in his synagogue. So, it was with much relief and admiration he heard Jesus simply rebuke the demon with the words, "Be quiet and come out of him."

Instantly the man fell to the ground. For a few seconds, he began writhing convulsively and shouting before becoming still. As the man stood up, he looked completely normal; in fact, he appeared positively happy and relaxed.

The people in the synagogue were muttering among themselves, and Jairus himself thought, *who is this man? He seems to have absolute authority over demonic spirits.*

After the service, Jairus approached Jesus and thanked him for the talk. As he looked into his eyes, he saw something remarkable: a mixture of calm confidence, yet kindness and approval.

"You must speak again," said Jairus. "I have never heard anyone speak with such profundity."

Jesus smiled and agreed to speak on another occasion before exiting the synagogue with his friends.

+++

Later that day, when the elder returned home, he was greeted by his daughter, who had witnessed the incident at the synagogue from her seat at the side.

"Abba, who was that man who preached? I really liked him."

"So did I," replied her father. "He made a lot of sense."

"Not like some of the rabbis you invite to speak," retorted Esther. "I can't understand much of what they say," she laughed mischievously.

"You mustn't be disrespectful," her father reproved, secretly agreeing with her.

"Who was that awful man who shouted at him?" asked Esther. "He really frightened me."

"Well, you don't need to be frightened by him anymore. Jesus seems to have restored him to his right mind."

"I wish I could see Jesus again. Do you think he would talk to children?" enquired the girl.

"I should think so" was Jairus' response. "He has such kind eyes. I have invited him to speak at our synagogue again."

Little did Esther know that she would encounter Jesus sooner than she expected and under some extraordinary, unexpected circumstances.

Chapter Three

THE HAZZAN, WHO was also the schoolteacher, was giving a lesson outside the synagogue. The children sat in a circle on the ground under some palm trees. Esther was one of the privileged girls to receive a synagogue education because of her father's position, so she sat amongst the boys.

The Hazzan asked the pupils to quote from the book of Leviticus, and knowing that Esther was likely to know a quotation, he pointed to her. But as he looked in her direction, he was shocked to see all the colouring had gone from her face. Unlike her usual confident self, she shook her head and he realised something was wrong.

Worried, the schoolteacher asked, "Esther, are you feeling unwell?" Esther was one of his favourite pupils, who always knew her scriptures well.

Although Esther's house was near the synagogue, the Hazzan thought it wisest for her to be accompanied home, so he turned to a boy sitting next to the girl and asked him to see her back. As she arose, the boy caught her arm just in time before she fell. Another pupil stood up and offered to help see her home, so together they propped Esther up and walked her slowly back to her house.

Two women were milling corn outside the house. Seeing the two pupils and Esther stagger toward them, they were alarmed. They jumped up in dismay and ran into the house to tell their mistress, who rushed outside.

"What is it, Esther? Are you ill?" she asked anxiously.

Rachel thanked the two friends and, placing her arms around her daughter, steered her through the main room, down a corridor, through a curtain, and into the girl's bedchamber. Esther flopped on her bed. She was shivering and her face had turned very white.

Rachel placed her hand on her daughter's head and exclaimed as she felt the burning brow. She shouted to the other women, who had followed them in, to fetch some water and a cloth. Then she asked them to send a messenger to bring the doctor. She sat beside her daughter's bed, mopping her brow and listening to her low moans.

The doctor, one of the local Pharisees, arrived quickly and examined the sick girl. Rachel told him her daughter had refused all food. He had a worried expression on his face as he said, "I will make up some potions to give Esther. Continue to keep her cool as you are doing, and I will come back tomorrow to see how she is."

Meanwhile the Hazzan had informed Jairus of his daughter's condition. Leaving his duties in the synagogue, he rushed home. When he entered her room, he was shocked to see his beautiful daughter lying so still on her bed. She will still dressed in her blue robe that suited her so well, but it was soaked with sweat, and Esther's eyes had lost their bright glow.

He knelt at the side of her bed and, taking her hand, spoke softly to her. "What is it, my daughter? How do you feel?"

Turning her head slowly and painfully, she formed the words through her dry cracked lips: "Abba, I have pain. Please help me." She searched her father's face for reassurance.

Jairus swallowed the fear that rose in his chest. Forcing a smile, he squeezed her hand and replied, "My daughter, Abba will find a way," as he tried to convince himself, but with very little hope.

Esther's parents took turns sitting by their daughter's bedside through the night and the following two nights.

During the day, Jairus had to attend to his duties at the synagogue, arranging and attending services, looking after the building, and maintaining the oil lamps. But as he was so near to his house, he was able to slip away at intervals to see how his daughter was doing. However, despite the doctor's potions, there was no change. Esther lay limp and lifeless on the bed, moaning softly and refusing to eat.

On the third day, Rachel met her husband as he entered the house at midday. She had tears in her eyes as she looked into his face. "She is slipping away, Jairus. What are we going to do?"

They raised their hands to Heaven and pleaded with God to heal their precious daughter. Suddenly Jairus heard a voice in his head: *Fetch Jesus.* It jolted him out of his sad thoughts, and he turned to his wife and exclaimed, "Jesus ... Jesus of Nazareth! Why didn't we think of him before? He heals people. Surely, he will come and heal our little girl."

"It's worth a try," responded his wife, "but I heard he has sailed to the other side of the lake, and nobody knows when he will return to Capernaum."

"No matter," replied her husband. Hope had sprung up in his heart. "If need be, I will hire a boat and search for him."

Giving his wife a quick kiss, he rushed out of his house and toward the shore of the Sea of Galilee.

Chapter Four

OBLIVIOUS OF WHO might be watching him, he lifted the skirt of his garment and ran as fast as he could. As he was descending the slope of the hill toward the beach, he spotted a fishing boat pulling into the shore. He shielded his eyes against the strong sun and thought he recognised the figure of Jesus stepping out of the boat.

Suddenly, as if from nowhere, the rabbi was surrounded by a swarm of people crowding and nearly suffocating him and talking at once. For a moment, Jairus felt sorry for Jesus. *He seems to get no peace,* he thought. *Wherever he goes the people throng him.*

When the crowd saw the tall, well-dressed determined figure of the elder, whose face showed agitation, heading toward them, they stepped aside to let him through. Flinging himself on the ground in front of Jesus, Jairus pleaded fervently, "My little daughter is dying. Please come and lay your hands on her. Heal her so she can live."

Jesus nodded and began to accompany Jairus, with the crowd pushing and shoving around him. He hardly had space to breathe, but his spirit had revived. He felt sure all would be well now. The presence of Jesus at his side somehow gave him hope.

But Jesus suddenly stopped in his tracks, turned round to the crowd, and asked, "Who touched me?"

Jairus was amazed, yet somewhat irritated, at the question. One of the disciples voiced his thoughts: "Jesus, everyone is touching you. How can you ask "Who touched me?" Ignoring the question, Jesus continued to look around the crowd.

Then the elder saw her. It was a woman he recognised. She had once been rich and was well-known in the town, but his wife told him she had become ill with some female complaint and used all her money on doctors, trying to get better. She reluctantly and with great embarrassment came and knelt at Jesus' feet, confessing she had touched the tassels of his outer garment.

By now Jairus was feeling agitated. Time was not on his side, and he listened with great impatience as Jesus told her that her faith had made her well.

It was then he recognised two of his servants rushing toward him, and his heart nearly stopped. "Oh no, please, God, no!" he prayed. He could see by the sad look on their faces that the worst had happened.

One of the servants spoke apologetically: "I'm so sorry, Jairus; Esther has gone." He looked at his master with pity in his eyes.

"You don't need to trouble the teacher. There's nothing he can do for your daughter now," the other man said.

A mixture of sadness and anger rose in him. *If only he hadn't stopped to speak to that woman,* he thought, *we might have been in time.*

As if knowing his thoughts, Jesus turned to Jairus and, looking reassuringly into his eyes, said, "Don't be afraid. Just have faith."

Despite his mixed feelings, there was something about the teacher's confidence that gave him renewed hope.

Meanwhile Jesus turned to the crowd and told them to leave. Muttering words of disappointment, the people backed away. He asked three of his disciples to accompany him with Jairus to his house.

As they reached Jairus' home, they could hear the incongruous sound of the professional wailers howling like dogs as flutes played melancholy music, and they found a score of professional mourners, with black hoods obscuring their faces, entering his house. It jarred on the father's nerves. Then, to his astonishment, Jesus spoke sternly to the women making all the noise: "Why all this commotion and weeping? The child isn't dead. She's only sleeping."

The women stopped wailing, and one of them spoke up. Jairus recognised her as the village gossip: "Don't be stupid. The child has died. We have been hired to cry for her." The rest of the women began laughing.

Jesus looked fixedly at them and said, "Leave this house. I only want those who believe present." Something about his manner caused the women to obey, and Jairus closed the door abruptly on the ritual mourners.

Then Jesus, his three friends, and Jairus went into Esther's bedchamber. Rachel, who was kneeling at her daughter's bedside, turned as they entered. She had tears in her eyes, and her cheeks were red and blotched with crying. Esther lay quite still with the whiteness of death on her face.

Jesus went up straightaway to the bed, took Esther's hand lovingly in his, and said in Aramaic, "Talitha Koum," which means "Little girl, arise."

Immediately Esther opened her eyes and Jairus noted with astonishment how bright they were as if nothing had happened. She got straight off her bed and ran to her father and mother. Then she turned to look at Jesus, who smiled as if they shared some secret, and, turning to Rachel, he instructed her to get some food for her daughter.

Jairus, who was trying to take in what had happened in just a few seconds, mused to himself: *The teacher is practical as well as a miracle worker*. Rachel, with her face glowing, nodded and asked Jesus if he and his friends would like to join them for a meal. However, the teacher replied that Peter's mother and wife had a meal waiting for them but that he and his friends would be happy to join them on another occasion.

Jairus turned to Jesus with such gratitude. "I don't know how to thank you," he stuttered. "You are certainly someone very special."

Jesus looked knowingly at him and replied, "You will have to be careful who you say that to, but it was your faith that led to this. Remember that."

With that, Jesus and his friends went out of the house, and Jairus was left reflecting, *could this be the expected Messiah we have all been waiting for?*

He thought of Jesus' words and remembered the visit from the two scribes after Jesus had healed the paralysed man. They had seemed intent on reporting the teacher, and the priest, Nathan, had seemed willing to take the news to Jerusalem. *What did they have against Jesus? How could anyone not see his goodness?*

He decided then and there to become a secret follower of Jesus, as he realised, he would have to keep his mouth shut for the time being. Jarius would wait until Jesus proclaimed his messiahship. Then he would confess his loyalty.

But of course, it didn't quite work out that way ....

Biblical references: Matthew 9:18–26; Mark 5:21–43; Luke 8:40–56

Say the Word

Chapter One

SEBASTIAN KNOCKED GENTLY at his master's door. Upon receiving no answer, he entered quietly. His master was asleep, so he moved silently round the bedroom, extinguishing all the lamps. He then returned to the servants' quarters for the night. He knew his master wanted an early start in the morning, so he would rise early and have his horse ready for departure.

As he prepared for bed, the young Greek slave boy sighed deeply. He felt very privileged to work for Centurion Celsus. His previous master had been so cruel. Sebastian experienced recriminations and beatings every week. So, the day Celsus bid for him was the best day of his life.

The centurion was a fair man, and although he demanded a high standard of service, he would show his gratitude when Sebastian or any of the other slaves worked well. This gave the young boy a great sense of loyalty so that he would do anything to please his master.

The next morning Celsus rose early. Sebastian had laid out his clothes for the day, so he slipped into his red linen tunic. The metal hanging strips of his leather military belt jangled as he buckled it round his waist. He would put on his plated armour and heavy red cloak after he had had his breakfast. Next, he strapped his feet into his heavy-duty sandals and moved out of his bedroom and into his living quarters where he found his breakfast already laid out for him.

As a soldier recruited from the Romans to join Herod Antipas' army, his job was to police the town of Capernaum and keep the peace. The Jews hated the Roman occupation of their country and there were often rumours of revolutionary movements. Herod was determined to stamp out any rebellion against his Roman masters who had put him in his position as tetrarch of Galilee.

Celsus and the soldiers under him had been garrisoned in Capernaum twelve years earlier. The centurion's commodious quarters were attached to the rectangular barracks just on the outskirts of town. Each morning he and several of his soldiers would ride out just as the people were heading for work, just to make their presence felt.

The Jewish people, hearing the clattering of hooves on the cobblestones, shied away in fear of the soldiers, as not all of them were as compassionate as Celsus. Soldiers were known to use their studded sandals to kick passing villagers who got in their way. However, the people had learned to recognise the centurion as the kindly officer who would not stand for any unnecessary violence, so they felt safe when he accompanied his men.

This morning, Sebastian was dutifully waiting with his master's horse. Celsus acknowledged his servant with a nod and a smile, donned his crested helmet, mounted his steed, and made his way through the streets of Capernaum until he reached the synagogue overlooking the Sea of Galilee.

He felt some pride as he approached the white rectangular building because he had made a substantial contribution to its construction. He loved the Jewish religion and had had many discussions with the elders and priests at the Capernaum synagogue.

Celsus had despised the Roman gods his parents taught him about when he was a child. They all seemed so immoral or cruel, and he had come to believe there was one supreme god who created everything, as the Jewish scriptures taught. One of the priests, Joshua, had become his particular friend, and he had discussed many of the Jewish scriptures with the centurion.

From these, Celsus had learned what a compassionate God Yahweh is and recognised that his laws made a lot of sense compared with the teachings of the Roman gods. So, it had given him great pleasure to offer to help build the community centre where the Jewish God could be worshipped, the scriptures studied, meetings of the community convened, and children educated. Even though as a Gentile, he could never enter the building or take part in its activities, he still had great respect for the people's religion.

He dismounted from his horse and handed the reigns to one of his soldiers. Celsus saw the priest coming out of the synagogue and approached him.

"How are you, my friend?" Joshua said, "How can I help you?"

Celsus explained that an order had come from the top that a carpenter who called himself a rabbi was attracting large crowds. This was always a concern to Herod and their Roman overlords because it suggested the "so-called" rabbi might be stirring up discontent.

Joshua took the centurion's arm and steered him away from the door of the synagogue where no one could hear them conversing.

"You must be talking about Jesus of Nazareth, he suggested, "but I don't think you need to worry about him stirring up trouble. On the contrary, he speaks only of peace, loving your enemies, and looking out for others. Moreover, he has the most amazing powers of healing. He healed a leper called Caleb, whom I diagnosed with leprosy twenty years ago. He came to see me a week ago and told me he had met with this Jesus who had completely healed him instantly. I have since heard the rabbi speak at this synagogue, and his teaching is revolutionary but not in the sense Herod thinks."

Celsus raised his eyebrows as he listened with some scepticism.

"I am told he has one among his number who belongs to the zealots. This does not sit well with my superiors."

Joshua looked furtively over his shoulder and lowered his voice as he spoke into his friend's ear. "He does talk of a kingdom, but I do not think this is a rival kingdom to Rome. In fact, I have been wondering if he is the servant of God we have been expecting, the one the prophets call the Messiah."

Celsus frowned: "But isn't he the one people believe will fight for them against the Romans?"

"That is the belief of some, but I have always believed when he comes, he will bring in a spiritual kingdom," Joshua replied. "But don't take my word for it. Why don't you find him and judge for yourself?"

"Where can I find him?" enquired Celsus.

"I believe he is not in Capernaum at this present time. He moves around a lot, but when he is here, he stays at the house of his fishermen disciples." Joshua indicated a large house a few yards to the south of the synagogue. "See, this is where the fisherman, Simon, and his brother, Andrew, live with their families. I will let you know when he returns.

"Send a servant to my house with a message when you know," requested Celsus.

"I will," responded the priest. But wait a moment." He disappeared into his house and came back carrying a scroll.

"This is the scroll of a man called Daniel." He passed the scroll to the centurion. "You will find this very interesting. It tells of the coming 'Anointed One' and gives dates for his arrival. I have studied those dates carefully, and I believe they suggest now is the time of the coming Messiah. You will have to use the old Jewish calendar I have explained to you to work out the dates. I will be very interested to hear if you agree with me."

Celsus grimaced. "I will certainly attempt to read this, but my reading of Hebrew is not very good."

"Oh, don't worry. This is written in the Greek version. I believe you know Greek?" smiled the elder.

Celsus's countenance brightened and he smiled. "Yes. I am fluent in the Greek language.

"Well, I will await your message. I bid you goodbye. May your God go with you."

With that the centurion retrieved his horse; mounted it; and, waving to his friend, indicated to the soldiers with him, who had waited patiently whilst he conversed with the priest, to follow him back to the barracks.

On the way back, Celsus became worried. The priest had suggested that the rabbi, Jesus, spoke of another kingdom. Even if he was the expected Messiah, he didn't think for one minute that Herod would appreciate his presence. He would see it as an attempt to usurp his role as king.

Celsus knew Herod was more interested in power than in God's will for his nation. He felt his loyalty was divided. His job was to serve the tetrarch as appointed by the Romans, but in his heart, he wanted only to serve the truth. He decided not to say anything to anyone about his conversation with Joshua until he had seen this rabbi for himself.

Chapter Two

IT WAS SEVERAL days before Joshua sent a message to Celsus to say the rabbi was back in Capernaum and once again staying at the house of his fishermen friends, Simon and Andrew. The message suggested he might locate the teacher on the shores of the Sea of Galilee, which he often frequented to give his teachings.

On Celsus' instructions, Sebastian saddled his master's horse and got it ready for him to mount. Again, Celsus took along with him a few of his soldiers. He didn't want to appear too intimidating; otherwise, the rabbi and his friends might get wise to his purposes. Nevertheless, he sheathed his sword on the left side of his belt and instructed the others to take theirs.

Arriving at the beach, he witnessed a huge crowd of people gathering on the shore and rode toward them. He saw fear on their faces as he approached, and the crowd scattered to let the soldiers through, although he did notice some defiant glances from some of the men.

He noticed a man with dark hair and a beard and wearing a rough tunic and outer garment with the customary fringes at the bottom. He was getting into a boat with some of his fishermen friends. This man he assumed to be Jesus.

Jesus began by telling a story about new cloth and new wineskins. As Celsus listened, he realised the teacher was saying new things were happening with his coming and the old ways of Judaism would have to adjust.

His voice was strong yet inspiring. The centurion found himself listening intently, impressed with what he was saying. He knew many of the interpretations of the Laws seemed ridiculous and made life more difficult for ordinary people, and he could see how some of the religious leaders might fear that Jesus would undermine their power. But then the rabbi went on to talk about loving your enemy and blessing people who cursed you. This did not seem to be the manner of a violent revolutionary.

At one point the rabbi looked straight at Celsus as if he were challenging him. But instead Celsus saw a look of deep concern on the rabbi's face and felt as if he could lay bare all his troubles to this man and know he was genuinely interested in him.

Celsus shook himself. He had to remember why he had come. His orders were to discern any note of rebellion or criticism of the present regime. So far, he did not feel any sense of threat, but he mustn't be taken in. Some of his men were becoming restless. So, he decided to leave, with a view to coming on his own next time.

Back in his quarters, at the end of a day of training his men, Celsus went into his dining room. As there were no windows and no skylight in this room, he lit some oil lamps.

Then he took out the scroll Joshua had lent him, spread it out on his large stone table, and began to read through the story of Daniel in captivity in Babylon. He was quite impressed by the wisdom of this Jewish man who had risen to the ranks of adviser to the king.

As he read on, he noted this young man's bravery in pursuing his religion in the face of Babylonian persecution.

He reached the part in the story where the angel, Gabriel, appeared to Daniel and told him of the coming of the "Anointed One." He gave some dates and events around this prediction.

Celsus took a papyrus and his reed stylus and began to write out the dates according to the ancient Jewish calendar, which Joshua had explained to him.

As he pondered the information on the papyrus, checking it back and forth against the scroll, he came to the astonishing conclusion that the dates worked out to the times in which he was living. He tapped the end of the stylus against his teeth

Hmm, Joshua was right, he thought. *This does seem to be the time of the arrival of God's special servant. But why haven't the Jewish religious leaders made this discovery?* he reflected. He would speak to Joshua about this the next time he saw him.

Chapter Three

IT WASN'T LONG before Joshua contacted Celsus to say that Jesus of Nazareth had been seen in the hillsides around Capernaum. Celsus dispatched a soldier to locate the rabbi's whereabouts, and when the soldier reported back, Celsus set off to find the rabbi.

This time he found the teacher on a hillside overlooking the lake. He was talking about two ways of life, about choice. He told a story about two builders, one who had built his house on a sturdy rock, which could withstand the elements, and the other who had built his house on a sandy foundation, which gave no support in bad weather. He knew Jesus was suggesting his way was the way of the rock.

This made a lot of sense to Celsus, and he decided then and there to trust this teacher and get to know his teaching further. He found himself intoxicated by the words Jesus spoke, and he noted, with pleasure, that when the rabbi looked at him, he seemed genuinely pleased to see him.

This time he waited until Jesus had finished teaching and was surprised to see the people lining up in front of him. There were cripples, blind people, mothers with crying children, others with gaping wounds, some even being carried on pallets. As Celsus watched, Jesus began patiently and gently touching each of the people and speaking comforting words over them.

My goodness, thought Celsus, *this could take hours. The line is so long.*

But Jesus didn't seem to tire, and he received each person as graciously as the next.

Celsus knew he would have to get back home, but he wished he could stay to watch this man, he now viewed with such admiration, continue to heal all the various complaints. This was certainly no rebel, a revolutionary perhaps, but of a kind the centurion wished there were more. He could certainly believe God had specially anointed this man and sent him to the people.

Celsus decided to stop at Joshua's house on his way home to discuss his theory. He found the priest crossing from his house to the synagogue and hailed him. The priest looked a little nervous as he approached.

well, I suppose, like me, Joshua has to be wary of speaking of Jesus for fear his superiors, the scribes and Pharisees, would find out, he mused. He knew, as a Gentile, he could not be invited into the priest's house, and equally he could not invite him to his own home, for Jews were not supposed to enter the house of a Gentile.

"Let us retire to the hillside behind the synagogue," whispered the priest. So Celsus dropped a shekel into the hands of a small boy passing by and, tying up his horse, asked him to look after the creature till he returned. It gave him great pleasure to see the expression of sheer delight on the child's face as he viewed his good luck.

The two men walked in silence up the hill. Lowering his body down onto the grass, the priest motioned to Celsus to do the same. "We will not be overheard here," he suggested. "Well, what conclusion have you come to, my friend?"

Flinging back his cloak, the centurion eased himself down next to Joshua.

"I have studied the dates and times in the scroll of Daniel, and I think you are right. It would seem to be the time for this 'Anointed One' to come." He considered carefully what he said next. "I have listened again to Jesus and watched his manner with the poor, sick people. He fits everything I would expect of a divine individual."

He waited for the priest to reply. Obviously, he too was weighing his words.

"I must be very careful not to give the impression that I approve of this rabbi. Only the other day two scribes came to see some of the elders and priests to ask us to report him. Apparently, he healed a paralytic who was lowered through the roof of Simon, the fisherman's, house whilst he was speaking and, they said, had the affrontery to offer to forgive the man's sins. The scribes thought it was a put-up job and wanted him reported to the religious leaders at Jerusalem for blasphemy."

"And do you agree?" Celsus frowned.

"I have watched this teacher carefully and listened to his message. It is true that only God can forgive sins. In my opinion, he is not only genuine, but I don't believe he would have said anything like that if he didn't mean it. So, there is only one conclusion I can come to."

The priest stopped and looked searchingly at the centurion to see if he had said too much.

But Celsus nodded in agreement. "That makes him the divine one himself. But I thought the Jews believe there is only one God." He raised his eyes enquiringly.

Joshua nodded. "Our scriptures recount several instances of 'The Most High' appearing as a man on earth. It is not beyond the bounds of possibility."

"Then he needs to be revered, not suspected and criticised," reflected the centurion.

Joshua looked intently into Celsus' eyes. "This conversation mustn't go any further than this," he pleaded.

"I understand," replied the centurion. "You have my word that I will say nothing of our talk. But thank you for being so frank with me."

He stood up and brushed the dry grass off his cloak. "I must be on my way. But I long to hear and see more of this teacher."

The two men walked back again in silence toward the synagogue. Celsus retrieved his horse from the young boy; untied it; and, mounting it, waved to the priest and cantered off.

Soon after this, a message from Joshua told Celsus that Jesus had left Capernaum again, and he would let him know when he returned. The centurion had time to ponder all he had heard the rabbi say, and he became even more convinced that Jesus had authority he could have received only from the Godhead.

Chapter Four

ONE MORNING, AS Celsus left his house for the usual excursion into Capernaum, he noted that his favourite servant, Sebastian, was not standing ready with his horse but another servant was holding the reins.

"Where is Sebastian?" he asked.

The servant replied, "Oh, did you not know, sir, the young lad is unwell? He was not able to leave his bed this morning."

Immediately Celsus ordered the servant to return the horse to the stables and informed the soldiers with him he was cancelling the trip to the town. He rushed to the door of the servants' quarters adjoining his. Inside the building, he entered a bedroom where there were several beds stretched across the room. A loud moaning sound directed his gaze to one in the corner. One of his servants was kneeling at the side of the bed on which lay Sebastian, whose tortured cries wrenched Celsus' heart.

"What has happened?" the centurion asked.

"Sir, Sebastian has been complaining of great pain in his stomach, but he says he cannot move his legs. He tried to get out of bed this morning to saddle your horse ready for your ride into Capernaum, but his legs just would not move."

"Send for a doctor." Celsus turned to another servant who had just entered the room. "Take my horse. Be as quick as possible," he ordered. He was distressed by the tortured cries of the man in the bed. He came close to his servant, and told the sick man, "I will do everything I can to help you."

Sebastian turned his bloodshot eyes toward his master in gratitude.

In a strained voice, he struggled to mouth the words, "Thank you, sir. You are the best master a man could ever have. But I have never had such pain in my life."

This difficult speech was followed by further groans that greatly distressed Celsus.

"Can I get you anything before the doctor comes?" he asked, feeling helpless.

The sick man shook his head and clutched his stomach as another searing pain shot through him.

Celsus instructed the other man to stay with Sebastian and promised he would return as soon as the doctor arrived.

It seemed like an age before the doctor came, and after he greeted the centurion, a servant showed him to the servants' quarters, followed by a very anxious Celsus.

"This man," he explained to the doctor, "has experienced much pain in his life and learned not to complain, so to hear him like this tells me he is very sick indeed."

The doctor examined Sebastian; asked him about his legs; shook his head; and, turning to Celsus with a worried frown, took him aside and said, "The man is paralysed from the waist down. Some blockage in his lower abdomen is causing this pain. I fear it is too late to save him."

"There must be something you can do," Celsus pleaded.

But the doctor shook his head again and reiterated his prognosis.

Celsus accompanied the doctor out of the quarters and into his own, where he paid him for his visit and asked a servant to conduct him out of the building.

Then Celsus sank heavily into his large wicker chair. The only thing he could think to do was pray. He lifted his hands upward and pleaded with almighty God, the God of the Jews, to help his dear servant. At that moment, he remembered Jesus. *Why didn't I think of him before?* he scolded himself.

He realised he could not ask the rabbi to come into a Gentile house, but he could send his friend, Joshua, and several other Jewish elders to ask for his help.

Celsus took from a drawer a piece of parchment and stylus and began to write a letter to Joshua, explaining that his dear servant was paralysed and tortured with pain. Celsus asked Joshua to take some of the elders, who knew how much Celsus had helped the Jews, to Jesus, to ask him to heal his servant.

Celsus folded the letter, closed it with his seal, and called for a servant to ride with haste to take the letter to the priest, Joshua. "Go as quickly as you can," he instructed. "I don't think Sebastian has long to live."

Back in Capernaum, at the synagogue, Joshua received the letter from his friend. He opened it, and after reading the contents, he called on two of the elders of the synagogue that he knew, like himself, respected the rabbi Jesus. One of them was called John and the other, Jairus. The latter said he knew where he could find Jesus.

It's just like Celsus to want to help a slave, Joshua reflected. He shared this thought with the others, and they agreed they would persuade the rabbi to help by telling him how much Celsus had done for the Jewish people out of love and respect for them.

They found Jesus coming out of Simon's house and immediately rushed to him and pleaded with him to heal their friend's servant. Jesus agreed readily to go with them to the centurion's house.

Back in his quarters, Celsus was restlessly pacing back and forth. He could hear Sebastian's groans rising from his bedroom through the connecting door, and it made him feel anxious. Yet he had faith that the rabbi would come because he had observed his great love and compassion for all the people who trusted him to heal them.

After some time, Celsus moved to the doorway of his house and peered into the distance to see if Jesus was coming. There he was, accompanied by his three friends from the synagogue and Jesus' disciples and, behind him, a large crowd clearly curious to see where he was going.

He looked as if he was intending to enter the house, but Celsus realised this would not be appropriate for a Jew and might land Jesus in more trouble with the authorities, so he called to him from the doorway. "Lord, do not trouble yourself by coming to my home. I am not worthy of such honour.

I am not even worthy to come and meet you. Just say the word from where you are, and my servant will be healed."

Jesus stopped, and Celsus saw the look of total amazement on his face but was also aware of the grumblings of some of the people in the crowd who were murmuring things like, "How does he expect the master to heal from here?" and "How ridiculous. He needs to touch the sick man. Why can't he bring him outside to Jesus?"

Despite the mumblings, Celsus continued speaking. "I know this because I am under the authority of my superior officers, and I have authority over my soldiers. I only need to say 'go,' and they go, or 'come,' and they come. And if I say to my slaves, 'Do this,' they do it."

He just knew in his heart that Jesus had such authority.

Jesus turned round to the crowd following him and spoke. "I haven't seen such great faith like this, not even among the Jews." Then turning to his disciples, he continued, "I want you to know this: many Gentiles will come from all over the world – from East and West – and sit down with Abraham, Isaac, and Jacob at the feast in the kingdom of Heaven, but many Israelites, for whom the kingdom was prepared will be thrown into the outer darkness where there will be weeping and gnashing of teeth."

Celsus could see this did not go over well with some of the men he guessed were spies sent to spy on the teacher. They looked quite angry and Celsus feared for Jesus' life. But for himself, these were the best words he could have ever heard.

This servant sent from God, the Anointed One, had truly come to bring his kingdom to the likes of him.

Then Jesus looked straight at the centurion and called to him. "Go back to your servant. You will find that, because of your belief, it has happened."

Celsus wanted to bow before Jesus and thank him, but the rabbi waved him on, so he rushed through the door and down the corridor, just as a servant was coming toward him, shouting excitedly, "He's better! Sebastian has completely recovered! Just now he got up, his colour came back, and he looks healthier than ever before. What happened? We were so taken aback. I have never seen anything like it."

Celsus told the man to bring Sebastian to him, and when he appeared, Celsus did something unheard of. With tears in his eyes, he embraced the young slave man and said, "Jesus of Nazareth healed you with a word. Don't ever forget it."

Biblical references: Matthew 8:5–13, Luke 7:1–10

A Lunch to Remember

Chapter One

EZRA STARED OUT of the window of the upper room of the house where he was staying. An old man now, he had been a member of "The Way" for forty years, but the memory of the miracle fifty years ago was as fresh in his mind as it was then.

He was ten years old at the time. As a reluctant sun was slowly edging its way over the horizon, sprinkling patches of light on the calm blue waters of the sea, he was playing with his friends on the western shore of the Sea of Tiberius, which foreigners called "The Sea of Galilee."

There had been a huge storm the night before, and the raging waves had carried debris onto the shore around the boys, littering the stones with dead fish, pieces of torn fishing net, and broken fragments of wood. It was hard to believe it was the same water. It seemed so self-assured as it lapped gently around their bare feet.

Fishing boats were returning after a night of fishing, many the worse for wear because of the storm. The muscular, deeply tanned fishermen tethered their boats and hauled their huge, much-mended nets over the sides, and dragged all their fishing tackle into weather-beaten shacks.

The boys were throwing stones into the water to see who could throw the farthest when they heard voices heading in their direction. A huge crowd of people surged toward them, some running and some walking quickly. Some were carrying the old and haggard on pallets, and others hobbled on one leg, leaning on wooden sticks. There were women carrying crying babies and an old, wrinkled, sour-faced man holding onto an equally frail, feeble, emaciated girl.

Ezra shouted to a young boy in a torn brown tunic, "Where are you going?"

He yelled back as he kept running, "To see the miracle worker. He's going across the lake to Bethsaida."

Bethsaida, Ezra thought. *It will take them at least six hours to get there and that's at a running pace.* But the idea of an adventure was too tempting to miss, and he had heard about the carpenter who worked miracles.

Ezra scrambled quickly up the hillside to his house, which sat at the top, overlooking the sea. Panting, he rushed inside, scattering the chickens that squawked indignantly. Calling to his mother who was baking some bread, he explained that he wanted to go with a crowd to see the miracle man at Bethsaida.

His mother's first reaction was to object that it was a long way to go and he wouldn't be back till nightfall, but he protested that there were a lot of adults in the crowd and he would keep close to them. So, being ever practical, she replied, "Well, you will need to take some food and water."

She filled a basket with five of her newly baked barley loaves and two small dried fish and covered them with a linen cloth. Ezra tucked the basket into a haversack along with a skin of water and, hastily waving goodbye, rushed out of the door and back down the hillside, followed by the protesting squawks of the chickens.

The crowd had increased in size, and they trailed for miles along the shoreline. Ezra ran to catch up and excitedly joined other children in the group, who, running at a fast pace, soon overtook everyone.

After two hours, the sun had made its way up the sky and beamed down on the crowd as if pleased. It was a pale watery colour circled with rings of light, and Ezra was enjoying its gentle heat. He looked across the sea at the shadowy hills beyond, where the mist was disappearing, and tried to imagine the layout of Bethsaida where the crowd was headed.

By midday, the sky had turned a bright blue colour, and the heat was so fierce the people were panting and dripping with sweat. Many were breathing hard, and some had stopped for a rest. The remainder of the shuffling, straggling procession stumbled on over slippery stones and through reeds, weeds, and sand, determined to complete the eight-mile journey to Bethsaida.

To cool their feet, Ezra and his companions paddled through some reeds at the waterside, startling a heron camouflaged by the grey reeds. It rose suddenly and flew off in search of its lunch. The boy had already finished the skin of water and wished he had kept some for later.

At last a relieved, exhausted mob arrived on the outskirts of Bethsaida. Because it was Passover time, the rolling hills were clothed in a velvety emerald-green blanket of grass, sprinkled with yellow-mustard flowers, interrupted by the occasional bright-red poppy.

Suddenly someone shouted, "There he is!"

Everyone turned their eyes to the lake where a boat was just coming in. Out of it stepped a man wearing a brown tunic and seamless robe. He was not very tall but had what Ezra observed 'an impressive gait.' He was wreathed in sunlight, and for a moment the boy thought he looked like an angel. He was followed by swarthy-skinned men, one of whom was tethering the boat.

Then the worrying thought struck Ezra: *Suppose he is angry that we have disturbed his peace?* But as soon as he saw the people his face took on an expression of such compassion. Stretching out his arms, he spoke words Ezra would never forget: "My sheep without a shepherd."

The man, some referred to as Jesus, led the way up a hillside, the weary bedraggled, footsore crowd straggling eagerly after him and his friends. He sat down and began to teach. Ezra stood, spellbound as he told one story after another.

Ezra had always loved the stories from the Torah, but these were new and referred to images from his daily life. He especially loved the one about a shepherd who went searching for the one lost sheep, because he found himself identifying with that animal, and instinctively knew this had a profound meaning for his future.

Chapter Two

WHEN JESUS HAD finished teaching, Ezra expected him to turn the crowd away and send them back to their homes. Instead, he invited the sick and disabled to come to the front and began laying his hands on their weak and feeble bodies. The boy watched in amazement as one after another the previously crippled and blind were jumping and shouting with joy because they were healed. Even the old sour-faced man Ezra had noticed earlier had a smile on his face. He had never seen anything like it.

The hours flew by, but Ezra was hardly aware of how the sun had moved around the sky. Some dark clouds appeared, and the light was growing dimmer. Jesus turned to a disciple to ask him where he could buy food. The man looked surprised and said it would cost a fortune to feed all these people. Then Jesus told his disciples to make everyone sit in rows. They moved around, organising everyone into groups, and they sat on the soft turf.

Ezra remembered his mother's provision of five barley loaves and two dried fish, and he was about to take out the small basket when he heard one of the disciples asking if anyone had some food to share. His stomach was rumbling.

His first thought was, *If I give up my food, I will be so hungry, so why should I? They should have thought to bring their own.*

He was sorely tempted to sneak off and devour his lunch, but another voice drowned out this thought. *No, if this man, who gave up his peace and quiet to attend to our needs, wants my food, then what right have I to be selfish and keep it for myself?*

Hesitantly he handed over his food, shocked to see no one else did the same. He did wonder if others had obeyed the selfish voice and kept their food for later.

As Ezra watched the teacher, he was filled with pride. Jesus took his offering and raised it to Heaven, thanking God for His provision. The boy's heart swelled. His small gift was God's blessing! Little did he realise how much of a blessing.

The disciples were carrying large baskets from their boats. They laid them on the ground in front of the teacher, making Ezra's small basket look insignificant.

What he witnessed next took his breath away. Jesus began dividing Ezra's mother's small loaves and fish into the baskets—yes, the baskets! Each one was filled to the top. He thought he must be hallucinating. After all, he was ravenously hungry. Perhaps the pain had dimmed his perception.

The disciples began passing the baskets along the rows as people grabbed handfuls. When it was Ezra's turn, he took out the equivalent of five loaves and two fish and ate hungrily, but so did the next person, and the next....

It must have taken a couple of hours for the disciples to distribute the food to everyone because there were thousands of people, and the kindly sun that had laboured all day was retreating slowly toward the west. Ezra felt satisfied and there were general murmurs of pleasure.

As Jesus dismissed the crowd, Ezra tried to process what had just happened. He had, after a struggle, given up his small lunch to the teacher, who had thanked God for the boy's gift and multiplied it till it became a blessing to everyone. Noone could possibly imagine how happy that made him feel? Even through this action, the rabbi was teaching him a lesson, one that would have a lasting effect on him for years to come.

As Ezra stood to leave, Jesus came towards him, carrying his small basket and smiling with such love in his eyes that the boy felt choked with happiness. All Jesus said, as he handed it to Ezra, was, "Blessed are the hungry, for they shall be filled."

Somehow, Ezra knew he wasn't speaking only of earthly hunger or bread and fish.

He watched with joy in his heart as Jesus and his disciples retreated into the hills, then ran to catch up with the rest of the people in the crowd, who, by this time, had lit some torches and were making their way steadily back to the shore. Darkness was coming fast, threatening to envelop the people, but Ezra's mind was full of light and elation. What a story he had to tell his family when he got home. Would they believe him?

+++

Now as the old man sat in his room, watching the flickering candle on the table in front of him and remembering that event, he wondered how different his life would have been if he had made the decision that day to keep his five loaves and two small fish to himself.

Biblical references: John 6:1–15
See also: Matthew 14:13–21; Mark 6:32–44; Luke 9: 12-17

The Cry

Chapter One

MIRIAM SLIPPED OFF her pallet as quietly as possible so as not to disturb her parents and sisters, who were still sleeping soundly. She opened the door and padded barefoot to the outside courtyard. The birds were beginning their joyful greeting of the morning as she climbed the steps. She gazed out over the flat grey buildings, observing other early risers on their rooftops, to where an early morning haze hung over the distant blue of the Sea of Galilee dotted with its tiny white sails.

A deep sigh rose within her as she thought, *I'm going to miss this town and all my friends. Still, I will only be about a day's journey away at Nain. Not so bad. And I'm sure I will soon make new friends.*

Miriam had been betrothed to Jonathan for nearly a year. She thought back to the day, just after her fourteenth birthday, when Jonathan and his father stood knocking outside their door. She knew why they had come—to establish a contract for Miriam's betrothal to her cousin. Her father had already asked if this was agreeable to her, and she had assented. Although she hadn't seen him for some years, she had played with Jonathan when they were children, and they had become best friends.

However, it was customary for the prospective groom to stand at the door and knock, and if the girl opened the door and let him in, that meant she accepted his offer of marriage.

Two neighbours had been called in as witnesses, and the two fathers sat to discuss the dowry Miriam's father would pay and signed three copies of the contract, the ketubah.

Miriam's mother had prepared the covenantal meal, and when they had eaten it, Jonathan and Miriam shared a cup of wine to seal the deal. Miriam looked shyly at her cousin as she drank. She thought him very handsome with his long, dark hair and neatly trimmed beard. He smiled warmly at her and she felt he was pleased. Her cousin's father then brought out some beautiful jewellery, and Jonathan gave the gifts to the delighted girl.

She hadn't seen the family since that day, although the parents had exchanged several messages to negotiate the arrangements for the marriage. Both Jonathan and Miriam had undergone the traditional washing ceremonies. A friend of Jonathan came often from Nain, with messages for his betrothed that were full of compliments, endearments, and wishes that the year would go quickly so they could be together. Miriam loved reading these letters. An excitement stirred within her as she read them.

But as she stood on the roof of her house, a new thrill of anticipation filled her. A year had gone by since that day, and Miriam realised that now that the barley harvest, followed by the ingathering of the wheat, and finally the summer fruit harvest had passed, Jonathan would be coming soon to take her as his bride to his father's house in Nain.

The girl had been to his family's house a few times when she was younger, and she knew it was on a farm where they grew barley and wheat. It was bigger than her home, with two extra rooms. She reflected that as a farmer's wife she would probably have to help with the chores on the farm, especially at harvest time.

Her reverie was interrupted by the voice of her mother calling her to come and help prepare breakfast. Since the betrothal, Miriam's mother had been teaching her daughter how to cook and take care of the household duties.

Her mother often commented, "Jonathan is a very lucky man. You will make a good wife for him." She sincerely hoped her mother was right.

"Coming, Mother," she replied as she ran down the steps and entered the house. The aroma of corn porridge greeted her nostrils as she took over the stirring of the pot from her mother, adding a little salt to the mixture.

She then fetched the malted grain cakes she had made the night before, and after lifting the heavy clay pot onto the table and placing there five cups of pomegranate juice, she called her sisters and father to sit down to eat.

Her father carefully rolled up the scroll he had been studying before sitting first at the table to lead the family in the grace recited before every meal: "Blessed art thou Oh

Lord our God, King of the universe, who bringest forth bread from the earth," he intoned.

Miriam's father was in the habit of reading from the Torah every morning before going to work. He was an earnest student of the Torah and had often sat his daughters on his knee and taught them how to memorise the scriptures. Miriam had always found it easy to commit to memory passages from the Torah, but her favourite story was about her namesake, the sister of Moses, who had watched over her baby brother in the basket as the Egyptian princess discovered their tiny secret. The first time her father had read the story, she held her breath as she wondered if the lady would kill the baby and sighed with relief when the princess decided to adopt him.

Miriam had often fantasised about being a beautiful princess, and she would soon have her chance to dress up for the week and wear all the jewels her cousin had given her. A tiny thrill of excitement went through her as she realised this could be any day now. Yet she also felt a tinge of nervousness at the thought of leaving everything familiar behind and living in a strange place.

Her uncle and betrothed would be busy preparing the bridal chamber.

As soon as it was finished, they would come for Miriam in the night.

No one would know quite when that would be, so each evening from that day on, Miriam would have to lay out her wedding robe and accessories. Her three sisters, who would be her bridesmaids, along with seven neighbours, were also keeping their robes ready, and everyone kept the oil lamps burning through the night. Miriam was finding it hard to sleep. She was so excited that her cousin could come for her at any time.

Chapter Two

AT MIDNIGHT THE triumphant sound of shofars and shouts of "Here's the bridegroom! Come out to meet him!" rang through the night, and Miriam and her family started at the sound.

"Quickly, they are coming," urged Miriam's mother.

Miriam arose, and with her mother's help, put on the beautiful white linen robe that had been her mother's wedding dress. Her mother had arranged her hair the night before, winding a plait round her long black hair that fell to her waist. Finally, trembling with excitement, she put on the headdress and veil over her head and placed a garland of flowers on top.

"I have saved this for your wedding day," her mother said, bringing out a small clay jar, and tipping the droplets on her fingers, dabbed the exotic-smelling perfume on her daughter's neck and wrists. It smelled intoxicating. Next, Miriam put on the necklaces, bracelets, anklets, and earrings her uncle had given her. Her mother looked at her daughter with admiration.

"Jonathan will be so delighted with you. You are so beautiful."

"I hope Jonathan will think so," Miriam replied. "When he lifts my veil, I hope he is pleased with what he sees."

Her sisters were also scrambling to put on their wedding robes when the other bridesmaids came rushing through the door.

"They are nearly here," her friend, Rachel said breathlessly. "The procession just passed my house."

Miriam felt a mixture of excitement and nervousness, as the exultant staccato of the shofars sounded nearby, and the girls rushed to the door of the house to greet the procession. They watched as the men, dressed in white finery, lowered the decorated litter with its white canopy to the ground.

Miriam peered shyly from behind her veil at the young eighteen-year-old man, who was dressed in splendid white clothing with a golden crown on top of his head, and looked even more handsome than before. Butterflies stirred in her stomach as he came toward her and, lifting her in his strong arms, carried her to the litter and sat her down.

Then began the singing of wedding songs, as four men raised the litter up on their shoulders. She was familiar with the words from the Song of Songs. "Who is this coming up from the wilderness like a column of smoke, perfumed with myrrh and incense made from all the spices of the merchant?" rang out the voices jubilantly as the procession moved off towards the father of the groom's house.

Carrying lighted torches and accompanied by shouting, dancing, and singing, the wedding procession moved through the streets as people came out of their houses to watch and cheer.

This is the best day of my life, thought Miriam. *I feel like a princess.* Yet underneath she felt a nagging doubt in her heart. *Will I be able to please my husband? Will I be able to adjust to my new lifestyle and be well-received by Jonathan's family?*

Eight hours later, as the sun was warming the hillside, the procession ascended the hill, along the path beside the terraced farmland shared by Jonathan's father and several other farmers, and arrived at the house. The procession was greeted by much cheering and clapping from the wedding guests, who were dressed in their wedding clothes and already enjoying the celebration.

The sound of pipes and drums echoed through the air, and the scent of the colourful flowers decorating the wedding bower and surroundings sweetened the atmosphere. As the groom's parents greeted Miriam and recited blessings over her, she sensed a warmth from them and breathed a sigh of relief that they seemed to accept her into their family.

However, it was still not time to complete the ceremony, and Jonathan's mother, Martha, showed the bride and her bridesmaids into another room whilst the groom joined the celebrations, which continued with dancing and games into the cool of the night.

+++

The following day Miriam was led to the decorated canopy and seated whilst professional musicians and singers played and sang traditional songs and blessings over her. She felt overwhelmed as the entire village had turned out to join in the celebration. Miriam was eagerly awaiting the arrival of Jonathan and felt a little guilty that she was glad when the songs and blessings ended.

Then she saw him, so tall and handsome, approaching the canopy. At last, she could speak to her husband. She held her breath as Jonathan lifted her veil. *I really hope he thinks I'm pretty,* she thought nervously. He smiled, and a warmth came into his eyes as he whispered, "You are so beautiful." She relaxed. This was the moment she had dreaded, but all was well. He loved her!

She had memorised her words from the Song of Songs that she was to recite to the groom. When she had finished, he responded with his memorised words. Now the guests began to shower gifts on the couple.

Then it was time for the prayers and blessings from the local synagogue leaders. At this point all the men joined their women to witness the rituals.

Miriam was feeling quite hungry, so she was glad when the father of the groom announced that the feast was ready. Once more she was parted from her groom as men and women were expected to eat separately.

The guests, having performed the ritual of ceremonially washing their hands with the water from stone jars placed ready, then reclined on couches round the three sides of the dining table on which was displayed large colourful fruit bowls of grapes, pomegranates, watermelon, dates, figs, and olives.

Three courses of culinary delights were brought to the table: a salad of mint, rue, coriander, parsley, chives, green onion, lettuce, colewort, thyme, green fleabane, and celery. This was followed by the main course of roast lamb and hot mint sauce.

Accompanying this were side dishes of chard made into a salad with lentils and beans, mustard as a green vegetable, and artichoke. The meal was completed with a dessert of pear compote made with dried pears boiled in wine and water together with honey, as well as dried apples mixed with toasted sesame. And of course, the wine flowed.

During the meal guests read poetry which offered blessings and good wishes for the future of the bride and groom and once more the professional singers sang to the wedding party, and more gifts were presented to the bride and groom.

Despite her hunger, Miriam could hardly eat anything because she realised that at the end of the feast the big moment would come. She worried; *Will I be pleasing to my new husband? Will he still love me at the end of the week?*

When the feast was over, she watched him approaching, and her stomach flipped. He took her by the hand and led her into the bridal chamber where everything the couple would need for the week, including food, was provided, as they would stay there for the next seven days.

Outside the chamber, the couple could hear the music and dancing as the celebrations continued without them.

Chapter Three

IT TOOK SEVERAL months for Miriam to settle into her new surroundings. After the wedding, her husband had gone straight back to working on the farm with his father, and Miriam was left to the supervision of her mother-in-law, Martha. She was a rather stern lady and had different ideas about housework than Miriam's mother had taught her, so she found herself making mistakes and displeasing her mother-in-law in the early days.

At the end of the day, whilst they waited for the men to return, Miriam would creep into the room she shared with Jonathan and silently shed tears. She was feeling very homesick and missing the companionship of her sisters. But Jonathan was a kind man and very gentle with her, and she didn't like to complain to him. He had to work long hours, so it took time for the couple to get to know each other.

However, as time went on, they were able to relax in each other's company. She enjoyed talking to him, and he was pleased that he could have intelligent conversations with her. They sometimes reminisced about their childhood days when they had played together. In the bedroom he was patient with his fifteen-year-old wife, and she, in her turn, was keen to please him.

Miriam was worried that she hadn't yet become pregnant. She knew how much Jonathan wanted a son, and Martha plagued her with questions each day about the possibility of a baby. So, it was with great relief that about six months into the marriage she realised she was at last pregnant.

Of course, there was great jubilation when she announced the news. A family friend brought the news to her family in Capernaum, and her mother and sisters visited with gifts of clothing they had made for the expected baby. Miriam also busied herself with sewing baby clothes, and Jonathan built a crib, which she lined with linen cloth.

Nine months later Miriam, with her mother-in-law acting as midwife, gave birth to a baby boy. Miriam was relieved that she had given her husband the son he so much desired, and as she looked tenderly into the face of her new-born, she thought, *He's so much like Jonathan.* They bathed the baby in water, rubbed salt into his body, and wrapped him in swaddling clothes.

When the baby was eight days old, the couple took him to be circumcised, and Jonathan named him Daniel. What a celebration the two families had on that day. Once more the wine flowed.

Daniel was a fairly easy baby, and Miriam received much help from his delighted grandmother in raising him. When he was two-and-a-half years old, Miriam weaned him. She had begun teaching her baby, and by this time she had taught him to memorise a text of scripture that contained all the Hebrew letters in his name.

As a Jewish father was bound to teach his son as soon as he could speak, something that often took precedence over eating a meal, Jonathan fulfilled these duties to Daniel, teaching him short psalms and scripture verses, wise sayings of sages, and simple prayers. Most of this had to be memorised as no written scrolls, apart from a few specially selected for children, were kept in the house. The boy was quick to learn, and his father observed that he had his mother's good memory, which secretly pleased Miriam.

When Jonathan lifted Daniel onto his shoulders, he became fascinated by the mezuza hanging at an angle to the righthand door jamb. The silvery decorative case that swirled around as Daniel touched it delighted the child and made him giggle. His father would open the case and read to Daniel the words of the Shema from the book of Deuteronomy, written on the tiny parchment scroll, and in no time the child could recite it back to him.

Daniel was intrigued by the little black box his father wore on his forehead each Sabbath to go to the synagogue. He would point to the phylactery, and Jonathan would take out the tiny scrolls containing the four passages of scripture from Exodus and Deuteronomy. He helped the boy make one for himself and taught him this was God's command to write His Law on his head and heart.

The family involved Daniel in all the religious festivals, and he learned much from watching the preparations and celebrations. His favourite was the Passover meal. He loved the excitement generated the night before when he and his mother searched for all the hidden yeast bread.

Every Sabbath, which began at sunset on Friday, Miriam, Jonathan, and Daniel, together with Jonathan's parents, attended the synagogue. The whole day was given to worship and relaxation, and all work ceased, so Jonathan had the chance to enjoy the company of his wife and son.

Daniel would watch his mother kindle the festal lights in preparation for each Sabbath. He listened as she recited the words, "Blessed art thou Oh Lord our God, King of the universe who has sanctified us by his commands and hast commanded us to kindle the Sabbath lights." His mother would bring in the incense, which filled the whole house with its fragrance.

His father would pour wine for everyone on the Friday evening and again recite the prayer, "Blessed art thou Oh Lord our God, King of the universe, creator of the fruit of the vine," which he taught his son to say. His father told him that after he died, it would be his duty to lead the family in this prayer.

Chapter Four

LIFE WAS GOOD and Jonathan's work provided for his family well. The work on the farm was hard, so at certain times of the year, Miriam helped her husband and father-in-law. She would take a basket and scatter the seed on the ploughed land.

Before Daniel went to school, he liked to accompany his mother. He would take handfuls of the seed from the basket and laugh delightedly as he threw it out, squealing excitedly as he shooed the birds away when they flew down for a free meal.

During the seven weeks of harvest, Miriam wielded a sickle to reap corn. One thing she loved about her husband was the generous amount of corn he told helpers to leave for the poor to collect. It reminded her of the story of Ruth, the Moabitess in the scriptures.

Often at midday, Miriam and her husband would sit in the shade of a makeshift bower made of four sticks hammered into the ground, with a rough roof of branches and sacking, and eat a lunch of pitta bread and boiled fish, followed by stewed figs or melon, whilst Daniel played with his toy donkey and cart a carpenter friend had carved for him.

Together they all enjoyed the festivities to celebrate the end of the harvest when they could take a break from the hard labour and enjoy feasting, laughing, and dancing.

+++

When Daniel was five, he began school at the synagogue where the teachers and pupils sat outside in a semicircle, and the children, taught by a synagogue official, learned to read and write from their study of the scriptures. Although everyone spoke Aramaic, the boys had all learned the Hebrew alphabet at home before starting school.

Daniel was able to read and write easy words in Hebrew, which prepared him for learning the Hebrew scriptures. The first scroll of scriptures Daniel was introduced to was Leviticus. From this he learned the customs and Laws that were to be part of his everyday life.

Being a sociable child, Daniel loved being with the other children, many of whom were his neighbours. Miriam was concerned that she hadn't had more children to give Daniel brothers and sisters to play with, and as the years went by, there was no sign of a further pregnancy. Miriam didn't like to seem ungrateful. After all, God had given her a delightful child in Daniel, and he was the apple of her eye.

But life was soon to bring its share of tragedies.

First Martha died of a heart attack. It happened so suddenly that there was no time to fetch a doctor. Then several months later, her husband also died. He came home one day with a fever, and the next day he had gone to his fathers.

Chapter Five

JONATHAN NOW HAD to take full responsibility for operating the farm and hiring workers, so he spent even longer hours away from the house, and with Daniel at school during the day, Miriam had to do the housework on her own and felt that her life was becoming quite lonely.

Meanwhile Daniel was growing into a tall, handsome boy. He was quick at learning and had memorised all of the Torah by the time he was ten. He was fluent in Hebrew and ready to learn the Mishnah.

When Daniel turned twelve, the age he was considered an adult, it was time for him to accompany his father to Jerusalem for the Passover celebration. Miriam didn't usually go with her husband to this occasion as the Law didn't require women to attend. However, this year they decided it would be good for her to travel with her son and husband.

Taking their animals for sacrifice, Miriam and her family joined a caravan of people also going to Jerusalem. It was fun for Miriam's family to join in the revelries of all their neighbours and friends. Like them many brought their best sheep and goats, whilst the poorer amongst them took caged birds.

People from other towns and villages joined them along the way, and Daniel made many friends amongst the other twelve-year-old boys also going for their first time.

When they arrived at the Holy City, they were struck by the business of the city vendors selling their rich varieties of food, foreign spices, and other goods. The noise was horrendous with the bleating of animals mixed with the cries of the sellers and music emanating from the temple. Miriam was aware of the Roman soldiers on duty, riding or marching up and down the streets, looking for any troublemakers. She found their stern expressions and cruel attitudes toward the poorer people intimidating.

Once the family passed through the "Beautiful Gate," Miriam stayed in the court of women, whilst Jonathan and Daniel went ahead into the temple to make their sacrifices. She found she was able to stand on her tiptoes on a raised platform to look into the inner courtyards and watch what was going on. There seemed to be much noise and business as the money exchanged hands and animals were bought and sold. It seemed a little odd to her that on such an important religious occasion there was little peace.

Life for Miriam seemed good again, so she was not prepared for what happened next.

Chapter Six

MIRIAM WAS HAPPILY sweeping the floor, singing a psalm to herself, when she heard a loud shout. One of the farm workers came rushing through the door, breathlessly yelling, "Come quickly, something has happened to your husband!"

Miriam's heart started beating wildly. She dropped the broom and, lifting her skirts, raced out of the house to follow the anxious worker. She ran as fast as she could along the hillside, her heart in her mouth. *What could have happened to Jonathan?* she thought.

She knew her husband had been ploughing his field that day, so she ran straight towards it. After about an hour they reached the field that belonged to Jonathan.

The farmworker came back to her and, taking her by the arm, tried to slow her down. "He had an accident," he said. "You must be prepared. I don't think he survived."

Miriam looked aghast at the man. "What are you saying? What happened?"

"He was ploughing the field, and we think he went ahead of the oxen to adjust the harness, but he fell over and hit his head on a sharp boulder. He must have passed out, but the oxen kept coming and walked right over his prostrate body."

Miriam gasped. Her heart raced. She was finding it hard to take in what the man was saying. This couldn't be true. Any minute now Jonathan would come toward her and greet her with his winning smile, and all this would have been just a dream.

But then she saw him lying on the half-furrowed field, blood covering his skull. She ran toward him and fell to the ground as she called his name, but his lifeless eyes stared back at her with no recognition.

"Fetch the rabbi doctor, someone!" she screamed, but her voice seemed miles away. She took Jonathan's hand, and it was as cold as ice. Now she began trembling. She put her ear to his heart, but it registered no sound. Then the sobs came. Her chest was heaving, and the sobs came thick and fast till she thought her chest would burst.

Suddenly she felt some strong hands pulling her up. She turned to see Daniel, who had tears pouring down his face. He pulled her to him and rocked her sobbing form.

"It's too late for a doctor, Mother. Father has gone to be with his fathers."

Miriam buried her head in the warmth of her son's chest. Then everything went black.

She woke up several hours later, lying on a pallet, in the dimness of a house. She looked around. It wasn't her house. Two small clay lamps were flickering. Then she heard the familiar voice of her friend, Sarah.

"Here, I have made you a drink. You passed out and Daniel brought you here."

Miriam looked blankly at Sarah and said, "Where is Daniel and why am I in your house?"

Her friend looked surprised. "He is seeing to all the arrangements."

"Arrangements? What arrangements?" Miriam was beginning to get flashes of images swirling in her brain: Jonathan lying on the ground, Daniel holding her. Then the realisation began to dawn on her. "He...he's dead, isn't he?" Tears began to course down her cheeks as her friend drew her into her arms and stroked her hair. "What am I going to do without my Jonathan, Sarah?"

Sarah struggled to comfort her. "Daniel will look after you. He is such a good son. Thank God, he gave you such a son. He will take over the farm and provide for you."

Chapter Seven

DANIEL HAD TAKEN complete control of the funeral arrangements and continued to be a support to his widowed mother. She found it so difficult to resume living her life. Jonathan had been her strength and she mourned his loss deeply. Her son now had to take charge over the operation of the farm, and although he was only seventeen, he proved to be a good manager.

Of course, he provided for Miriam, and in time she was able to go on living her life. She made sure to thank God every day for giving her such a good, loving son. She knew only too well what would have happened to her if she no longer had a man to support her. She would have lost all inheritance and ongoing financial support and been reduced to poverty.

+++

With Daniel now managing the farm, in time Miriam resumed her household duties. Sometimes she would accompany her son to market, and she went back to helping at busy times on the farm. At times when she felt a little gloomy, she pondered how life would have been if she had been left without anyone.

One ray of hope came when Daniel, at nineteen, chose his future wife and asked his uncle to help him arrange the betrothal. She was a second cousin to Daniel and lived in Tiberius on the Sea of Galilee, about twenty-one miles from Nain. Miriam had met the girl, Deborah, only once, but she had taken to her on that occasion and began to look forward to having some female company in the house again.

Memories of her own betrothal to Jonathan and the arrangements came flooding back as Daniel related to Miriam the details of his and his uncle's visit to the girl's house. She vowed she would treat the girl less harshly than her mother-in-law had treated her.

She is fortunate to be getting Daniel for a husband, Miriam mused. The future looked so much brighter now, and Miriam began to sing again as she worked. She was even looking forward to grandchildren when fun and laughter would fill the house once more.

Miriam was humming to herself as she prepared a meal when she heard the shuffle of feet outside. The sheep and goats were making a lot of noise and, putting down her broom, she went to the door. To her surprise, Daniel was slouching toward her with laboured steps. His face was white, and he called out to her in a pained voice.

"Mother, I don't feel well. I need to lie down."

Miriam clasped her son round the waist and helped him into the house.

"What is it, Daniel? You look so pale. What happened?"

"I don't know," he replied in a hoarse voice. I suddenly came over weak. I haven't been feeling right for several days."

She helped him into his bedroom and laid him on his pallet. She felt his head. It was burning hot. Fear seized her.

"I will send for the rabbi at the synagogue," she muttered.

The boy had closed his eyes and did not respond.

Miriam rushed to pour some water into a clay basin and, dipping a cloth in it and wringing it out, she placed it on her son's head.

"I will ask someone to fetch the doctor." She didn't want to leave him but needed to find help quickly. "I will be back as soon as I can."

Reluctantly she left the boy's side and rushed out of the door, causing the animals to scatter. She found a boy playing outside, offered him a coin, and told him to run as fast as he could down the hill to the synagogue to fetch the rabbi.

After returning to Daniel's side, Miriam again soaked the cloth in water and held it to her son's brow. She stayed there, mopping Daniel's head until the doctor came, but he remained silent.

After a brief examination, Rabbi Saul shook his head. "There isn't much I can do for him," he said. "He has a fever. Just keep him cool as you are doing, and I will return tomorrow to see if he is any better."

Tears sprang into Miriam's eyes and silently she pleaded, "Oh God, don't take my only son from me. Please, please let him live."

She stayed by her son's side the rest of the day, only leaving him to renew the water in the basin. He still hadn't spoken and refused to eat.

Midnight came and Miriam began to nod off, shaking herself awake from time to time to return to mopping Daniel's brow, but his body felt like a furnace and he didn't open his eyes. Eventually her head dropped unto his chest, and she fell asleep.

The crowing of a cockerel woke her with a start. Daniel's body felt cold beneath her head. She looked at her son. His eyes had opened but they were staring blankly.

"No!" she screamed and placed her ear to his heart, hearing nothing. She took his hand. It felt like ice. All hope drained from Miriam, and she fell to her knees, feeling numb. A voice stirred her to go and get help, so she forced herself to rise and run out of the house to Sarah's, the next farm on the hillside. She screamed as she entered the house, "He...he's dead!"

Sarah took her in her arms to comfort her. "I'll come with you, and you can tell me what happened," she soothed.

Sarah had been talking to a farmhand from the village, so she quickly told him to run to her husband's land and tell him what happened, and the two women returned to Miriam's house.

When Sarah saw the rigid figure of Daniel lying on his pallet, she fetched a linen shroud and covered his body. Miriam was shaking and sobbing and sitting beside her prostrate son when Sarah's husband, Michael, rushed in. He put his hand compassionately on Miriam's shoulder and said, "I will see to all the arrangements. We will need to have the funeral tomorrow before the Sabbath begins."

Miriam nodded numbly. She felt as if her heart had splintered into a million pieces.

Sarah stayed with her friend and helped her wash and anoint her dead son's body. Miriam worked like an automaton. "I will arrange for other women in the town to prepare the meal of condolence," Sarah said.

Other neighbours started to arrive to express their sympathy for their friend.

Miriam couldn't show any emotion or gratitude and was quite relieved when they left.

Sarah stayed with her friend until the evening, but Miriam refused all offers of food. When Sarah eventually left, Miriam flung herself on the ground, sobbing inconsolably.

All night long Miriam lay on the floor, sobbing and crying out to God, "What am I going to do now? You took my husband, and now you have taken my only son."

+++

Thirty-seven miles away Jesus of Nazareth was praying on the hillside of Capernaum, surrounded by his disciples. In his spirit he heard the cries of the poor widow.

He got up and woke his disciples. "We need to start walking. We have to get to Nain by the morning."

The bleary-eyed disciples looked puzzled, but they knew better than to argue with the master. So together they set off on the long journey.

Chapter Eight

T RUE TO HIS promise, Sarah's husband had made all the arrangements for the funeral, and in the morning, Sarah came to Miriam's house. She roused the exhausted woman and helped her wash and anoint the body with spices in preparation for the procession.

Four men from the neighbourhood came and lifted the pallet where Daniel lay.

When Miriam stepped out of her house, she was greeted by several of her neighbours and friends who had gathered to join the procession. Some women had begun the traditional wailing and flute-playing, and Miriam found herself becoming irritated by the noise but was too polite to say anything. Every nerve in her body was taut, but having wept all night, she felt she had no strength left in her to cry, yet tears insisted on flowing down her cheeks, unhindered.

She walked with her head down. The shattered fragments of her heart seemed to jar within her. It felt as if life had ended for her.

As they reached the bottom of the hill, more people from the village joined the procession. They stopped on several occasions to recite psalms, though Miriam didn't have the strength or will to join in.

Just as the procession reached the village gates, it suddenly came to a halt. Miriam looked up in surprise to see the four men lower Daniel to the ground as a man accompanied by a crowd was approaching.

She was about to ask why they had stopped when the man came toward her and looked straight into her eyes. His eyes were filled with compassion and, as he spoke softly to her, his voice was full of warmth, "Don't cry."

In that instant, she felt pure love flowing into her heart like a stream of liquid gold, uniting the severed parts. This man knew exactly how she felt, and somehow, he was going to make everything all right.

He turned and walked over to her son. The people gasped as he touched the dead body and said, "Young man, I tell you, get up."

Miriam watched in amazement as Daniel opened his eyes and sat up, looking round curiously. "What's happening? Where am I?" He stared at the crowd in bewilderment. Then, seeing their astonished faces and looking down at the pallet on which he lay, he realised what was happening. Jesus took his arm, helped him up, and led him to his mother. Mother and son embraced hungrily for some minutes. Then, as they parted, Miriam turned to thank the stranger, but he was nowhere to be seen.

"Where did that man go?" she asked the people in the crowd, who were still shocked by what they had witnessed, and were talking excitedly and praising God, but they shook their heads and muttered, "He just seemed to disappear. We don't know which way he went."

"Who was he?" asked Miriam.

One man stuttered, "He must be a great prophet."

Another man raised his hands to Heaven and said, "I believe God has come to us today."

The whole crowd began to talk at once, so Miriam couldn't make out what they were saying. Then a voice from the crowd spoke loudly, "Do you think he could be the Messiah we have all been waiting for?"

There was a sudden hush. Then Miriam responded, "I have never seen anyone look at me like that before. Such love, such compassion, such God-like presence! You are right. Almighty God heard my cry and has come to us today! I need to find him and thank him for what he has done."

Daniel placed his arm round his mother's waist and spoke softly, "We must certainly find him, but right now I need to get you home. You look exhausted. I have lots to tell you about what happened to me when I died."

With that, he picked up his pallet, and everyone headed back to their homes, singing and dancing as they went. The funeral had turned into a great celebration.

Biblical reference: Luke 7:11–17

Delivered from Darkness

Chapter One

LUKE WOKE UP to the sound of yelling. Nothing unusual, just his father shouting at his mother...again. This had been the boy's experience since he could remember. He pulled his cover tightly over his head and tried to block out the sound. He was trembling and praying to any god he could think of, "Please don't let my father come to me," but either the gods did not hear this piteous cry, or they didn't care, for the next minute he heard the heavy footsteps of his burly father crashing into his room.

"Get up, you lazy, good-for-nothing!" boomed the man's voice. He yanked off the covers and began kicking the boy, who recoiled in fear as he struggled to get up. "Get to work now!" bellowed the big man. "And don't come home till you bring us some money."

Luke hastily pulled on his tunic and ran quickly out of the room. As he passed his mother, she crammed a barley cake into his hand. He retreated out of the house and, with tears flowing down his face, ran down the street. He thought back to the only pleasant memory he had of his mother cradling him in her arms when he was a baby, gazing at him with such love. "I love you, Luke," she would say, and he felt the love trickle into his heart and warm it.

But his father was so cruel and controlling. He beat his wife frequently and not a day went by that, in a state of drunken fury, he laid into Luke and berated him with curses. His mother was so frightened that she was unable to protect him, and the light and love went out of her eyes as she struggled to keep sane each day. Sometimes when Luke was younger, his father locked him in a dark, dusty cupboard and left him there till night-time where he would sit filled with fear and anger, seeing no hope for the future.

Things changed even more for the boy after his mother died, when he was just ten years old. She had been worn down by her husband's treatment of her and grew very sick with a fever. After her death, Luke's father became even more deranged and cruel and somehow blamed the boy for his wife's passing.

In his heart, the boy decided that one day, when he grew up, he would kill his father and run to safety. He felt the world had done him no favours, and his heart became calloused with murderous thoughts. As far as he was concerned, there was no love or help in the world. One day he would get his revenge on it and everyone in it.

Eventually, when he was thirteen, Luke escaped from his home and aimlessly wandered the streets, stealing food, until he fell in with some other disaffected youths. He frequently joined in with the others when they beat up their victims and left them for dead. As he kicked a man to death, all he could think was, *why should he deserve anything better than me? All he could feel was hatred* and anger. He felt that life had let him down and he didn't want anyone else to know happiness.

But beneath that hard exterior was a gnawing doubt that there was another way. The memory of his mother's loving eyes had become dimmed, yet it came back to him at times, especially in the night, when he was alone with his thoughts. At such times he knew there was another way, but it was only a faint glimmer.

Something fearful happened to him one night as he lay in bed, unable to sleep. Voices began to speak to him, urging him to "Kill, kill, kill." One voice whispered, "You are mine now. You will never be free." Luke began to feel heavy and depressed and from then on could get no sleep. Sometimes he would scream out in agony and cover his ears to block out the sound, but the voices just got stronger. If he did go to sleep, he would wake up in a cold sweat, seeing in his mind the old man he kicked to death, lying in a pool of blood as the voices laughed maliciously.

Try as he might he could not replace this image with that of his mother's smiling face whispering, "I love you, Luke." Somewhere at the back of his mind was a flicker of hope that there was love to be found, but the voices mocked this thought and filled him once again with hatred and murderous ideas.

The tortured man began to run wild in the streets, screaming obscenities at everyone he met and lurching threateningly toward them. The other boys cast him out of their gang, calling him a "complete madman."

One day he heard the clang of boots behind him and turned to see two Roman soldiers. They quickly threw chains around him and hauled him off to prison.

As he sat, chained to a prison wall, a huge rage grew like a seething monster inside. He felt as if thousands of forces were driving his body, and an enormous strength, like a raging furnace, filled him so much that he ripped and tore at the chains until he broke free.

He rushed out, blood dripping from his arms and legs as he pushed open the prison doors. A guard blocked his way, so Luke smashed down on the guard's head with the metal attached to his arms; knocked him to the ground; and fled the building, ranting and raving. He felt himself ushered toward the local graveyard where he began howling like a wolf until he fell asleep behind a burial cave.

Many times, after this, he was rearrested and returned to prison, but each time he broke his shackles and went rampaging round the cemetery. No one was strong enough to subdue him, and in the end, the Roman soldiers gave up trying to arrest the madman.

Chapter Two

SCREAMING AND SPITTING anger, he ran toward the hillside. The chains, which had bitten into his wrists and ankles, tore into his flesh till he was dripping blood. Eventually he reached a cave in the hills, and for a while he became calm again. He sat down to contemplate his fate. It was clear that he could not return to the town. He would have to remain in the hills and forage for food.

But his mind was seething with mental agony, and he found himself reaching for sharp rocks, cutting into his flesh to try to assuage the mental pain. He tore at his clothes, leaving himself completely naked. But all this did was increase the torture and leave him bleeding and scarred. He wished he could die, but night and day the voices tormented him relentlessly. "Kill, kill, kill," they hissed. There was no peace to be had.

When anyone came by, he would surge into an unbelievable rage and plunge toward them so that they ran in fear whilst he screamed curses after them. After that, no one dared come near him.

That was his life for years. He lost all sense of time. He found some quiet moments in foraging for food and drank from a stream. The unnatural strength from the demons inside him enabled him to kill wild animals with his bare hands and devour the raw meat like a wild beast.

On one occasion he had returned to the graveyard and was coming out when he looked in the direction of the Sea of Galilee and spotted a fishing boat heading toward the shore. There appeared to be four or five men in the boat, and as they pulled it onto the shore at the foot of the hill, a Jewish man with a beard and dark shoulder-length hair stepped out, accompanied by the other men and began ascending the hillside. He felt compelled to rush toward the man shrieking in an agonised voice. "Why are you interfering with me, Jesus, Son of the Most High God?" Luke asked. "I beg you, don't torture me."

Luke didn't know why he said this, but the man was calling to him.

"Come out of him."

The Jewish man was looking straight at him, and his eyes penetrated in such a way that he felt overpowered with his strength, yet at the same time, he remembered that maternal love he had experienced as a baby. Luke felt as if the man was sending a flow of soothing liquid love through his body, and he sensed it was torturing the demons inside him. He felt weak at the knees as the man spoke with a calm, yet authoritative, voice, "What is your name?"

The wild man opened his mouth to reply, "Luke." But what came out took him by surprise. "Legion," he retorted in the gruff, sinister voice he had become accustomed to. In that instant, he realised he was inhabited by a multitude of demons.

Again, he was astonished as he took on a pleading, wheedling voice. "Please, please don't send us to some distant place. Send us into those pigs. Let us enter them."

The man he had referred to as "Jesus" replied, "GO!"

As Jesus spoke, Luke felt as if his whole body was being torn apart, squeezed, and violently crushed as he was thrown brutally through the air. He fell with a resounding thud on the ground.

As he lay there, the most incredible wave of peace cascaded through him. A mixture of joy and happiness swept into his heart. He lay exhausted whilst he witnessed a herd of pigs rushing down the hillside, plunging over the cliff nearby, and making a huge splash as they descended into the water below.

Luke lay as if in a dream and was vaguely aware of the man directing the others with him to clothe him. They began to lift him gently and pulled a tunic over his naked body.

The man he somehow knew was called "Jesus" reached out his hand, and as he gently raised Luke to his feet, Jesus looked into his eyes with such an expression of love that he responded in his heart with a deep love for him, something he had never experienced before. He felt that he wanted to follow this man to his death. Jesus began to speak soothingly to him, urging him not to be afraid. He talked of His Father, God, who loved him and wanted him to be his disciple.

By this time a crowd had gathered. They had been alerted by the herdsmen, who had run screaming that the pigs had drowned. Many of them obviously recognised Luke and looked positively fearful, amazed by what had just happened. They made it clear they wanted Jesus and Luke to go as far away as possible. They were afraid of what this Jewish man would do next. They walked away, shaking their heads and muttering obscenities.

Jesus and his friends turned and began to walk down the hill toward the boat. Luke rushed after him, pleading in a normal voice that took him by surprise. He so desperately wanted Jesus to take him with him. He felt so safe in his presence and was fearful that if he left him, the demons would return.

But Jesus turned; shook his head; and, looking straight into Luke's eyes with the most beautiful, yet stern, expression said, "You have an important job to do here now. You must return to your people and tell them all the Lord has done for you. They will believe you because of how much you have changed, and they need to know about God's mercy."

Luke knew then he was looking into the face of a god, but it wasn't any of the Greek gods his mother had taught him about when he was a child. He had never fully believed in them. This was the God he had heard the Jews speak about— the one and only true Creator God. He realised he owed it to him to tell his people everything.

That is how he came to preach throughout the region of Decapolis, where he lived, and witness to the crowds, who, fearful at first, recognised who he was and were astonished at the change in him. He won them over by his quiet demeanour and shared with them what God had done for him, urging them to believe the one who delivered him was the only true God, who had power over the devil and all his demons.

Biblical references: Matthew 8:28–34; Mark 5:1–20; Luke 8:26–39

Unlocking The Light

Chapter One

JAMES WAS BORN blind. When he was old enough to talk, he would constantly ask his parents why he couldn't see what everybody else talked about, but they couldn't give him an answer. People had to describe what things looked like. As a small child, when he asked what made everything so hot, they described the sun as a big red ball in the sky, and he pictured a large version of a bouncy ball they gave him to play with, glaring down on him from above.

James' father was a potter, and he would lead him into his workshop and place a ball of clay into his hands. He loved to squeeze it, enjoying the soft squelchy texture. Then later his father would hand him a finished pot that had been fired in his kiln, and he marvelled at how the clay had been transformed into a solidly shaped jug or bowl as he traced the curves with his fingers.

Because he couldn't see, his other senses were well-developed. He was aware of many sounds around him every day: the harsh bleating of sheep and goats, the raucous cries and shouts of children playing, the pleading voices of traders selling their goods, and the rattle of the heavy iron wheels grinding on the cobblestones. He knew when the Roman soldiers were approaching by the clattering sound of horses' hooves, followed by the harsh, commanding voices of the men on horseback and the frightened cries of people kicked out of the way.

He could discern the disgusting stench of dung mingled with all sorts of sweet, spicy, and savoury food smells.

He learned to feel his way around the streets where he lived, by touching the rough basalt stones of buildings. Each one felt slightly different. People laughed at him when he stepped in the dung that was everywhere in the streets, and they cruelly remarked how disgustigly smelly he was. It was so hard to avoid treading in it.

One thing he loved was to plunge his face into the soft, curly, wool of his favourite goat, drink in the warm aroma of his body, and sometimes even confide in him all his deepest burdens.

James wasn't able to read, but even when he was very young, his mother and father read to him from the Torah, writings, and prophets. Fortunately, he was able to memorise most of the scriptures, but his favourite was toward the middle of the scroll of Isaiah where the prophet talks about the One who was coming who would open the eyes of the blind. He held on to the hope that he would live to witness that day.

As he got older, he had to beg on the streets. People would drop money into his bowl. He learned to tell, by the different metallic sounds, which coins were being dispensed. Most of them were the small copper lepton that wouldn't buy him much unless he collected a number of them. On rare occasions, charitable people would drop in a didrachma or even a shekel. That would be a very special day for James.

He wasn't aware of any of the religious leaders giving him money. He knew they were nearby because of their derisive remarks about what a sinner he was to have been born blind. Sometimes unkind boys would kick his begging bowl away, laughing maliciously as he crawled around trying to retrieve it. At times he would feel around inside the bowl only to find all the money was gone.

Some kind people occasionally brought food to James, but most days he sat for long hours without anything to eat or drink. It was a very lonely existence as hardly anyone spoke to him.

On the great festival days, James' parents would take him to the Jerusalem temple to sit on the steps whilst they went into the courtyard to make their offerings. Because he was disabled, he wasn't allowed anywhere near the temple courts.

As he sat listening to the sound of animals bleating mixed with traders yelling, the rhythmic lisp of sandal straps, the excited conversations among thousands of people brushing by him, and the relentless racket of carts and wagons, he became aware of the smells of animal dung contrasted with the sweet smell of frankincense wafting from the temple.

He could also distinguish the voices of the religious leaders from the common people. They would make disparaging remarks about him and other beggars as they passed by suggesting that his blindness was the result of his sin or the sin of his parents. It was hard for him to believe God was punishing him for the sins of his parents before his birth. They were good people, albeit very poor, and they did their best for their son. However, he knew he would never be able to work like normal people and help them. So, life went on in its monotonous way, day after day, with little hope of any real future ahead.

On previous visits to Jerusalem, James had discovered the stone steps leading from the temple to a sacred pool, the pool of Siloam, a place where people went to cleanse their bodies before a religious celebration. Some would use the many mikvehs near the temple for this purpose, but others preferred to immerse themselves in the deep pool under the ground, which was served with water from King Hezekiah's tunnel. It was a long way down, and James trailed his hand down the cool, moist rock, his faithful stick leading the way to the bottom.

He traced his direction to the pool by the echoing sounds of voices bathing. It gave him such pleasure to immerse himself in the refreshing water, splashing the silky liquid on his face, soothing away the troubles of the day.

Chapter Two

IT WAS WHEN James' parents went up to the temple in Jerusalem for the Feast of Tabernacles that the miracle happened. He had been sitting on the steps leading up to the temple for seven days in the blazing heat, whilst people excitedly talked about building their shelters.

The air was heavy with animal stench as people brought their sacrificial offerings. He was surrounded by the bleating of sheep and goats, the tweeting of birds in their cages, and a medley of strident voices of sellers mixed with the raucous bellowing of cattle. Below the temple steps were sounds of shrilly bargaining shoppers as well as the harps and pipes of travelling minstrels. The strong smells of incense, spices, and aromatic and medicinal herbs wafted toward him.

On the final day, he felt a sense of peace as many of the sounds had ceased and were replaced by the joyful sound of the Levite choirs singing in the temple. He had been told to wait till sunset when his parents would fetch him to return home.

Suddenly his silence was interrupted by the sound of voices approaching and he held out his bowl hopefully toward the sound. Some men seemed to be discussing the young beggar. He recognised the strong Galilean accent as one asked, "Rabbi, why was this man born blind? Was it because of his own sins or his parents' sins?" James felt enraged by the question. What business was it of theirs anyway?

Then another voice, quiet, yet haunting, spoke. He sounded so confident in what he said, but it was what he replied that caused James' heart to rejoice. "It was not because of his parents' sins or his own sins."

These were the words the young man had waited all his life to hear. He felt as if a huge load was suddenly lifted off him.

The man, he now assumed to be the rabbi his friend had addressed, continued. "This happened so that the power of God could be seen in him. We must quickly carry out the tasks assigned to us by the one who sent us. The night is coming, and then no one can work. But while I am here in the world, I am the light of the world."

Wow, James thought *this man is something different*. Although he didn't fully understand all that the rabbi said, he knew it sounded very special.

What happened next took the young man completely by surprise. The rabbi knelt beside him, and he heard him spit. Then with a deliberate, gentle touch, he rubbed some sticky cold substance, James guessed was mud, on his eyes. He jolted as the dirt seeped grit into his eyeballs.

Then the rabbi helped James to his feet and said, in a friendly but authoritative voice, "Now, go and wash in the pool of Siloam."

James couldn't help but muse that the meaning of Siloam was *sent* and this man had mentioned something about "being sent." Was there some connection? Whatever it was, He felt driven to obey his instructions.

Feeling his way down the cool stone steps leading to the pool, James was careful not to slip, as the stones had been wetted by many feet ascending from their bathe.

The gritty mud was irritating his eyes, so he was relieved when, after about fifteen minutes, he reached the bottom of the many steps. Voices were echoing all around him as he imagined people staring at this beggar man with mud on his eyes.

He pulled his robe above his head and, stepping down into the pool, submerged his body in the deliciously smooth waters, splashing them up toward his eyes. He continued until he felt all the mud had been washed away. As he opened his eyes, he gasped. He found himself looking at greyish shapes floating in the green water. He stared in disbelief at a reflection of his own face.

As he stood up, he saw the tall stone walls surrounding the pool, and was aware of shadowy shapes that gradually morphed into more solid forms until he could distinguish the bodies of the bathers. A silence had descended upon them as they stared at him in amazement. This blind beggar, who, previously, had to feel his way around, was jumping up and down excitedly shouting, "I can see! I can see!"

Tears began to wash down his face as the full realisation of what was happening dawned on him.

Now he found his way by sight to the bottom of the stone steps and began his joyful ascent to the top. He had to find that man and thank him. Who was he? How did he choose to heal him?

Chapter Three

AS JAMES EMERGED into the sunlight, he was stunned by the cacophony of colours surrounding him. Above him wispy white fluffy shapes floated in a beautiful sea of azure blue. Multicoloured robes and headdresses of red, purple, yellow, and blue passed him by, and as he gazed around, he was impressed by the whitish-brown stones of the many rectangular buildings glittering in the sunlight, and the thousands of recently erected booths lining the streets, People, animals, birds in slatted cages were everywhere, and he could see faces clearly—old, wrinkled faces; young, keen features.

Everywhere were mounted patrols of Roman soldiers, and for the first time, he could observe the severity of their expressions. He could see why people were frightened of them.

Then James noticed men dressed in finer black robes with long tassels at the hems and what he supposed were striped prayer shawls draped around their shoulders. He realised these were probably the Pharisees and scribes, as they walked importantly down the steps from the temple, and people stepped aside to give them room.

He stared up in amazement at the grandeur of the holy temple, rising seventy feet into the sky. The hot sun, shining on it, made it look more elaborate and magnificent than he had imagined. He knew he was looking from the South side and could see the court of the Gentiles leading into the court of the women. He gazed in awe at the porticos, towering columns, and staircases.

On a previous occasion, James' parents had taken him round the outskirts. He could feel the stone walls and had some idea of how large the temple was on the outside. Of course, he had never been allowed to enter it as he was considered unholy because of his blindness.

He began to ascend the hundreds of steps to the temple, asking people as he went, where the man was who had put mud on his eyes. People were staring at him in astonishment, some obviously recognising him as the blind beggar they had previously observed on the steps of the temple.

They were discussing his appearance, some saying, "Surely this is the blind beggar who sat outside the temple every day."

Others remarked, "No, it can't be. It is just someone who looks like him." James tried to shout to them that he was that man and he had been healed, but they weren't listening.

He was anxious to find and thank the rabbi who had healed him, but when he reached the outer gates of the temple, and enquired as to his whereabouts, no one seemed to know where or even who he was.

Suddenly he found himself encircled by a haughty procession of black-robed figures who blocked his way and aggressively began to ply him with questions. "Are you the man they are saying has been healed of blindness?"

"Yes," he replied.

Whereupon they marched him off to a building where other men, he assumed were Pharisees and scribes, were assembled. Roman soldiers were standing guard at the doorway, and their intimidating stares followed him as he was practically thrown into the room by the religious leaders.

These religious leaders began to grill him further, pointing out that it was the Sabbath day and according to the Law the man should not have been healing. James thought it a little strange that someone who only blessed him was being criticised for his actions, but he knew the religious leaders had some severe interpretations of the Law of God.

He told these Pharisees that a man had put mud on his eyes and told him to wash it off in the pool of Siloam. Immediately after he did that, he could see. However, he was annoyed that they didn't seem pleased for him and instead started proclaiming, "That must have been that man, Jesus, who disobeys the Law all the time. Clearly, he is not from God." This made him feel quite indignant because that man had shown more care for him than these religious leaders.

A few of his inquisitors did make the comment that it seemed strange that God used the healer to do something good if he was a sinner, and James fully agreed with that sentiment. However, they were shouted down by the others and it caused an argument amongst them. James just wished they would leave him alone.

All he wanted was to find this Jesus, thank him, and then return home and surprise his parents. But they insisted on plying him with questions such as "Who was the person who healed you?" and "What did you think about him?"

Clearly, he was a prophet and James told them he believed this. They seemed very annoyed by his answer, and after they inquired who the young man's parents were, they went to find them. This didn't take long as they were on the steps to the temple, enquiring about their son's whereabouts.

As the elderly parents were dragged into the court, James' mother exclaimed joyfully when she saw her son with his eyes clearly seeing. James started to tell his story to them, but one of the Pharisees rudely interrupted, speaking abruptly to his parents, "Is this your son? Was he really blind?"

"Was he blind from birth?" another intercepted.

James' astonished parents looked at each other in puzzlement. They were clearly frightened and embarrassed by the manner of the religious leaders.

"Well, yes this is our son, James," replied his father. "He has been blind from the moment he was born, but how he can see now, and who has healed him we have no idea." The religious leaders were looking so perplexed, and James longed for them to just go away and leave them in peace so he could celebrate his newfound sight with his family. But on and on they questioned them.

James' father was becoming exasperated with their questions and retorted rather sharply, "He's a grown man. Why don't you ask him yourself?"

The Pharisees became quite menacing, suggesting that if it was the so-called Jesus of Nazareth whom some said was the

Messiah, he was not of God because it was against the Law to heal on the Sabbath. James could see his parents were too scared to say anything more. They were afraid they would be excluded from the synagogue if they spoke well of this healer.

The Pharisees took James aside roughly and implied that he should denounce this "so-called healer" as a sinner and give the glory to God for his healing. *Well,* thought James, *of course I give God the glory,* but he also felt the man called Jesus should receive some credit, so he replied rather brusquely, "Look, I don't know if the healer is a sinner or not. All I know is that I have been blind all my life, but now I can see."

Even that wasn't enough for them. "Explain to us. What did he do to you?"

Well, that was too much for the young man. He exploded. "Look! I told you once. You are not listening to me. What's with all these questions? Do you want to become his disciples or what?" He knew he sounded rude, but they were really trying his patience.

Then these so-called "religious leaders" actually cursed James! *How dare they?* he thought.

One of them said, "More likely you are his disciple. We are Moses 'disciples. We don't even know where this man came from."

"Well, that is very strange," James interrupted. "All I know is that he definitely healed me, and it has always been my belief that God doesn't listen to sinners, but he does listen to people who worship him and do his will." He looked point-edly at the men. "I have never heard of anyone opening the eyes of a person born blind, so this would seem to say this Jesus is from God." He stared at them defiantly.

This, of course, angered them further. They became very red in the face, and one shouted at James aggressively, "You are a sinner—born a sinner—and you will never enter a synagogue again." And with that, they threw him out of the court, along with his parents, leaving them all quite speechless.

Chapter Four

THEY STARTED ON their way home, but James had the strong feeling he was being followed, perhaps spied on. He was hoping to encounter the healer again when a voice spoke behind him. "Greetings, James."

Recognising the calm, friendly voice, he turned round to see a man with shoulder-length dark hair and a neat beard smiling at him. He too was wearing a prayer shawl and suggested a commanding presence, yet he had reassuring eyes, and his demeanour was quite different from the crowd who had questioned him earlier.

"I am the one who healed you, James. I heard you were being interrogated by some of the religious leaders. I'm sorry you had to go through that."

He looked at James fixedly. "Do you believe in the Son of Man?" he asked.

James wasn't sure what he meant, so he replied, "I want to, sir, if I knew who he is." He had a vague recollection of his parents teaching him that the title "Son of Man" in the scroll of Daniel spoke of the coming Messiah.

The rabbi, whom James assumed was the Jesus the Pharisees had mentioned, replied, "You are looking at him, and he is the one speaking to you. "James felt overwhelmed with a kind of joy mixed with reverence and fell to his knees in an attitude of worship. "Yes, Lord, I believe," he whispered.

As Jesus continued to tell James he had come into the world to bring judgement, to give sight to the blind, the young man recalled his favourite passage from the prophet Isaiah and realised his dream had come true. The one of whom the prophet had spoken had come, and was looking straight at him.

When Jesus had finished speaking, James noticed a couple of Pharisees listening in on their conversation. They accosted Jesus, "Are you suggesting we are blind?" they asked angrily.

It was only then that James grasped the double meaning in what Jesus had said.

Jesus turned calmly to them, and James couldn't help smiling to himself complacently as he replied, "If you were blind, you wouldn't be guilty, but you remain guilty because you claim you can see."

James knew then that he was looking into the face of the expected Messiah and promised himself then and there to follow him.

Little did he realise then what it would mean for him, when not long afterwards, as he learned about Jesus' crucifixion and resurrection, he joined the people of "The Way," and that was when life really began for James.

Biblical reference: John 9:1–41

The Misfit

Chapter One

A SHORT, STURDY, bearded man of about forty years sat with his head in his hands, his goblet of wine untouched. He couldn't remember the last time he felt happy. He seemed quite oblivious to the raucous conversations around him or the loud singing in one corner of the inn.

He thought of all the wealth he had amassed: his huge Roman-built mansion and his thousands of denarii in the bank. He had everything he wanted, yet he was dissatisfied.

Zacchaeus'mind recalled his childhood when, as an only child of wealthy parents, he had been indulged and spoilt. He had not taken much notice of the teaching on the scriptures at his synagogue school; in fact, he did not have much time for God or religion at all. But he was a clever student and very quick with mathematical calculations.

His one ambition was to become wealthy. He was small of stature, and the other boys bullied him and made fun of his size. This made him even more determined to make good and laud it over others to compensate for his height.

When his parents died, leaving him a sizable fortune, he decided to become a tax collector for the Romans. He knew this meant bidding for the job at auction. The Roman official, called the Censor, would look for the person who tendered the lowest rate of commission, so this is what he did and found himself, at the age of twenty, the local tax collector for the city of Jericho.

After serving his five-year contract, he managed to ingratiate himself with the Censor and was appointed chief tax collector of the region.

Like most tax collectors he frequently cheated the taxpayers and extorted more money than he had a right to so he could pocket the difference and he had no conscience about taking bribes from rich citizens to let them off paying their full share of taxes.

It was no wonder the ordinary people hated him. He was not only regarded as a collaborator with an alien government, but people knew he was cheating them. Yet they had no recourse to complain because he would threaten to report them to the Roman officials for not paying.

Everywhere he went he was greeted with evil looks. People would mutter under their breath as he passed by, "Dirty, lousy sinner; traitor. He has no right to live."

He would ignore their comments and smile to himself, thinking of how much wealthier he was than they.

However, despite his riches, he was not satisfied. There seemed to be a gaping hole in his life, which he could not put a name to, a heaviness of heart that plagued him day and night.

He was tired of his lonely existence. No one ever came to see him except for business purposes, and they would come and go without exchanging any cordiality with him. He rambled around his large four-storey mansion with its mosaic-floored living and dining room, on his own, with only the servants to share the space. He wasn't even pleasant to them, keeping them at the lowest wage he could pay and making selfish demands of their time.

He stared round the inn at the groups of people talking and laughing. All of them seemed to be having a good time except for him in his solitary existence. How he longed for some friends. Of course, the innkeeper was polite to him, but he knew this was only because he was a good-paying customer.

His attention was arrested as he overheard the words "tax collectors" mentioned at the next table where a group of traders were enjoying flagons of wine and chatting heartily. He leaned closer, and trying to block out the surrounding cacophony of noise, strained to hear the conversation.

One man was holding forth to his companions. "They say that carpenter, Jesus of Nazareth, is travelling through tomorrow. Apparently, he is on his way to Jerusalem."

Another interrupted, "He's that religious man who fraternizes with tax collectors, isn't he? The Pharisees don't think much of his behaviour. They think it isn't very proper for a man who claims to be religious."

His friend added, "I believe one of his best friends was a tax collector in Galilee. He really isn't very particular."

The first man replied, "Yes, but the rumour is that he works all these miracles. He heals people of leprosy and all sorts of conditions. Maybe we should get a view of him. It is rumoured that he is travelling to Jerusalem and should arrive here tomorrow. Personally, I've never seen anyone perform a miracle. Might be an interesting sight to see," he added.

Zacchaeus had pricked up his ears at the mention of "tax collectors." A religious man who ate and drank with the likes of him—that was novel. His curiosity was roused. What made this man so interested in someone other people despised?

Although he was due to visit a particular tradesman to collect his taxes the next day, he decided to take the day off and watch for this rabbi.

Zacchaeus plucked up the courage to speak to the men at the next table. As he waddled toward them, they stared at him with contempt. He was well-known in Jericho, but avoiding their stares, he addressed the first man who had spoken. "Excuse me. I heard you mention Jesus of Nazareth. Do you know how far off he is from Jericho? When would you expect him to arrive here?"

"You think he'll want to see you, your dirty lousy sinner?" He laughed and his companions joined in the derision with contemptuous laughter.

Zacchaeus decided to ignore their mockery and persisted. "I'm just curious to see if he is as clever as they say he is."

"Then you'd better get yourself down to the gates of the city early tomorrow morning, but don't expect anyone to let you anywhere near the man."

Zacchaeus nodded and retreated to the door of the inn, accompanied by sneers and scoffing from the entire assembled company.

It was the ninth hour when Zacchaeus arrived at his house. With his wealth, he had bought a beautiful Roman domus with landscaped gardens and lagoons at the Southern boundary of Jericho. Inside were marble pillars and fresco-covered walls.

He was met by his porter, who unlocked the studded wooden door for him. He had scores of servants for whom he showed no respect, and now he called for one of them to prepare his evening meal before he descended to the lower level to take a bath and change his clothes. All the time he was thinking, *who can this man be who eats with tax collectors? I wonder if I can just get a view of him to see what he is about.*

Chapter Two

THE NEXT MORNING the little man rose early from his comfortable bed, and dressing in his silk tunic and embroidered overcoat, he hastily devoured his breakfast a young servant had brought to his room.

He stopped at the door to give the porter instructions, then hailed a carriage to take him to the gates of the city.

Descending from the carriage, he paid the driver and noticed a crowd of people already gathering at the gates. In no time the crowd had increased to several hundred, and it was so dense that Zacchaeus began to despair of getting anywhere near the carpenter man, realising that because of his height, he would be unable to get a good view.

Then an idea came to him. He had passed a sycamore fig tree with low branches further down the road. Perhaps he could climb it and get a better view as the crowd passed by. He looked around for the carriage driver, but he had already left, so ignoring the indignity of his position, he lifted the skirts of his robe and ran as fast as he could to get well ahead of the others. In the distance he heard the shouts. "There he is! He's coming!"

Everything in him yearned to see this Jesus. He wasn't sure why, but he felt as if it was the most important thing in his life at that moment.

When he reached the tree, he quickly shinned up it and sat on a low fork, trying to hide behind the thick layer of leaves.

As he spotted a dark-haired bearded man leading the crowd and walking with a kind of self-assurance in his manner, his heart began to race. At least he would get a good view from here, he thought.

The crowd was getting closer and he could clearly see the man's face. It was strong, yet calm, and there was a determination about the way he moved.

Then he stopped. Zacchaeus held his breath. Would he see him? Would everyone laugh at this pompous little man crouching in the branches of a tree? But Jesus was looking straight up at the tax collector, staring right into his face. The crowd was shouting abusively at him, but Jesus held up his hand and instantly they ceased!

Zacchaeus found himself looking into the most profound eyes. And somehow, he felt Jesus was seeing right into his soul. It made him feel somewhat uncomfortable when he realised what he would see, and yet at the same time, he sensed this man understood and accepted him completely.

Then, to his astonishment, Jesus spoke in a friendly, entreating voice, "Zacchaeus."

How does he know my name? he thought. *He isn't from around these parts.*

What he said next nearly catapulted him out of the tree. "Come down quickly. I want to come to your house today."

Zacchaeus scrambled enthusiastically out of the tree. He could hardly believe his ears. No one had ever wanted to come to his house as a friend, yet this stranger was willingly inviting himself! To the jeers and insults of the people, he set off with Jesus to his house.

As they walked along the road, the little man found himself pouring out his soul, admitting how lonely he felt, how depressed. His words came tumbling out as he admitted all the cheating, he had been involved in. He was thinking, *I'd better let him know the truth. Then if he doesn't want to come home with me, it will save me the embarrassment when he finds out.* However, Jesus was listening intently as if he wanted to hear every word, as if he valued all Zaccheus was saying.

The porter looked astonished when he saw Jesus accompanying his master, and when Zacchaeus stopped to ask his servant to prepare a meal and drinks, she gave him a suspicious look.

He led the way down a windowless corridor, lit by torches on the walls, into the atrium, the open central court at the centre of his house. It had an open roof, which let in light, and a shallow pool sunken into the floor to catch rainwater from the roof.

This spacious room was decorated with elaborate statues and plants, which gave it a refreshing outdoor feel. Zaccheus indicated to Jesus to recline on one of the couches whilst he sat on the one opposite.

As he continued his saga of deceit and theft, he found himself dissolving into tears. He surprised himself. He couldn't remember crying since his childhood.

When he finally stopped talking, Jesus looked at him with such compassion and asked, "What do you want to do now, Zacchaeus?"

The tax collector knew exactly what he wanted to do. Somehow this man with his compassionate eyes and total acceptance of this lonely soul compelled him.

"I will give half my wealth to the poor, and I will restore fourfold all that I have stolen," he blurted out.

Smiling at him with such love in his eyes, Jesus said, "Today, salvation has come to this house, to you, Zacchaeus, who is a son of Abraham."

"Son of Abraham." The little man was astonished. He was used to people telling him he had given up his rights to become a Jew. He questioned why he was so privileged, and Jesus replied, "The Son of Man came to seek and to save those who are lost."

The tax collector felt overwhelmingly relieved, cleansed, and happy. All the anger, hurt, and revenge had left his heart, and he felt utterly forgiven. In just a few hours this man had given him back his self-respect and peace.

When the maid came to bring the meal, she saw immediately a change in her master as he spoke kindly to her and suggested she take the rest of the evening off.

Zacchaeus was true to his word and immediately began to give money to the poor of the city and to restore to all those he had robbed fourfold what he had taken.

+++

That is not the end of the story. Soon after his encounter with Jesus, when the little man learned about Jesus' crucifixion and resurrection and the formation of "The Way," he sought out Jesus' followers and joined them. He was one of the early Christians who led the way in selling everything he had and sharing with the others.

Biblical reference: Luke 19: 1-10

THE CHILDREN BROUGHT TO JESUS
A Sketch

Characters: Disciples, at least two: Simon Peter and John. Number depends on actors available.

Jesus, mothers and children – one boy is a cripple with a homemade crutch.

Reference: Mark 10:13–16

(Jesus and his disciples enter)

John: Jesus, you are looking very tired. So many people again. You are so patient! We should find a quiet place to rest for the night.

Jesus: We will go up this hillside and rest.

(Noise of mothers and children coming toward Jesus and his disciples. If this is performed in a church, they could come down the aisle. They could all be chatting at once, children shouting, babies making crying noises.)

First woman: Come here, Jonathan (calling to a boy). We are going to see Jesus. He will bless you.

Second woman: I hope he will heal my baby. She won't stop crying.

Third woman: Look, there he is. Come on, let's catch them up.

Peter (intercepting them): Where do you think you are going?

Fourth woman: We want to see Jesus to ask him to bless our children.

Peter: Not so fast. The master has had a long day. He is much too tired to see you.

(Women mutter disappointment)

First woman: Oh, but this is our only chance to get Jesus to bless our children. Surely he will see them.

Peter: Go to your homes. You can see him another day, but come a bit earlier next time.

Jesus (overhears Peter and approaches him): No, Peter! Don't send these dear people away. Let the little children come to me. Don't stop them. You know the Kingdom of God belongs to such as these. (Smiles at the children and, as he speaks, picks up a little child in his arms.)

(Peter looks annoyed, shrugs his shoulders, and walks toward the other disciples.)

Jesus (crouching down to the level of the children): Come with me (He takes the hands of the leading children and moves centre stage).

(He begins to pick up the children one by one and places his hand on their heads as he speaks.)

Father, bless your little one and keep him/her safe from all harm (and variations of this).

(When he has blessed all the children, he sets the last one down and draws a little crippled boy to him. He gently takes the boy's crutches away and tells him to try to walk. The boy takes a few tentative steps, then begins to run around and back to Jesus. He hugs Jesus' knees. Jesus turns him to face the adults, his hands affectionately on the boy's shoulders.)

I tell you the truth, unless you change and become like little children, you will never enter the Kingdom of Heaven. And whoever welcomes one of these children welcomes me.

(He points to all the children and looks sternly at the adults.)

Be assured that if anyone harms one of these little ones, it would be better if a millstone was tied around his neck and he should be thrown into the depths of the sea.

(General gasps and murmurs from the adults.)

(He gathers all the children together and hugs them).

(The children return to their mothers and start to go off as they all speak at once. Jesus watches them with a loving smile on his face.)

First child: Goodbye, Jesus.

(The others repeat this, waving to Jesus as he smiles and waves back.)

Jesus (turning to his disciples): Now let's find that quiet spot for the night.

(They exit.)

Why Me?

A Poem

1.My tortured mind
Seethes with thoughts
That besiege the battered brain.
Soul sick with pain,
And there's nowhere to hide
Except in suicide.
Why me?

2. He prays as he bows the knee
In the dusk of Gethsemane.
Soul crushed with grief and pain
With the flow of bloodied sweat,
And yet....
He bowed his head and said,
"Not my will, but Thine."
Why, God?

3. JUSTICE HAS FLED
AND LEFT ME SORE.
THERE IS NO DOOR OF ESCAPE.
TWELVE VOICES WITH DERISION
MADE THE DECISION
ON FALSE EVIDENCE.
THE JUDGE GAVE THE SENTENCE
THAT SEALED MY FATE.
WITH HEAVY HEART
I HEARD HIM SAY,
"TAKE HIM DOWN ...
AND HANG HIM."
WHY ME?

4. BEFORE HIS UNJUST JUDGES
THE GALILEAN PROUDLY STOOD
AND WOULD NOT
SAY A WORD IN HIS DEFENCE
AGAINST THE PRETENCE
OF WITNESSES.
AND YET WE HEARD THE CRY,
"CRUCIFY! CRUCIFY!"
WHY, GOD?

5. I AM ALONE,
REJECTED, ABANDONED, BETRAYED.
MY SO-CALLED FRIENDS LOUDLY CONVEYED
THEIR DISPLEASURE AS A MEASURE

OF THEIR LACK OF FAITH IN ME.
NOW I SINK BENEATH THE FLOOD OF TEARS.
MY FEARS
OVERWHELM ME,
FOR I SUFFER THEIR DISLOYALTY.
WHY ME?

6.EVEN HIS CLOSEST FRIENDS
DESERTED HIM AT THE END.
AND IN HIS MOMENT OF NEED
THEY SELFISHLY SLEPT WHILST HE WEPT.
HE FELT REJECTED,
DESPERATELY UNPROTECTED
BY THE LOYALTY OF FRIENDS.
EVEN ONE DENIED
HE KNEW HIM
TO HIDE HIS OWN FEARS.
SO, HE WALKED THE PAINFUL PATH ALONE TO
THE CROSS.
WHY, GOD?

7. MY BODY IS SEARED WITH PAIN.
THE CRUEL CANCER RESIDES
IN MY BONES,
AND WITH FIERCE FINGERS CLAWS
AT MY INSIDES,
UNTIL I CRY WITH PAIN
AGAIN AND AGAIN,

PLEADING FOR RELIEF.
BUT NONE COMES
TO SOOTHE MY ACHING BONES.
WHY ME?

8. THEY WHIPPED HIM TILL THE SKIN,
TORN AND BLISTERED, PEELED.
HE REELED AS THEY THRUST
HIS SKINLESS BACK TO THE WOOD.
AND HE COULD
FEEL THE JANGLE OF NERVES
AS THEY PIERCED HIS HANDS AND FEET.
AND HE TRIED TO CONSERVE
EVERY BREATH—AN AGONY OF FLESH.
HEAD THORN-TORN THAT BLOODIED HIS FACE
TILL THERE WAS NO TRACE
OF THE ORIGINAL.
LEFT IN THE SKIN-SCORCHING HEAT,
WHICH GNAWED LIKE A LION AT THE MEAT
OF HIS BODY.
WHY, GOD?

9. I AM ALL ALONE.
MY WIFE DIED AT MY SIDE
AND LEFT ME TO LINGER ON
IN TROUBLED TORMENT OF DESPAIR.

And no one seems to care
I am bereaved,
Lost, beside myself with grief.
Why did Death deal
Such a fatal blow?
The pain of loss has shattered my soul.
I am alone forever.
Why me?

10. At that moment when he poured
From dry and blistered lips,
"My God, My God,"
The psalmist's words
Woefully wrenched from his heart.
"Why have you forsaken me?"
"Abandoned me to the grave?"
And all his being heaved with
The loneliness of despair.
Not even love was there.
Drenched in the sin of the world.
A filthy carcass upon whom God
could not bear
To look.
Why, God?

11. He has left my room,
Taken my soul.
Now an empty tomb.

ALL THAT WAS PRECIOUS TO ME:
MY HOPES, MY INNOCENCE, MY TRUST,
AND NOW MY GUILT,
MY YOUTH ALL SPILT,
THRUSTS ITS UGLY FINGERS INTO MY HEART
THAT CRAWLS LIKE MAGGOTS IN THE DUST,
AND I AM LEFT TO LIVE
WITH THE BITTER TASTE OF SHAME,
NEVER TO FORGIVE AGAIN.
WHY ME?

12. THEY STRIPPED HIM OF HIS ROYAL ROBES,
LEFT HIM NAKED AND EXPOSED.
NO DECENT LOIN CLOTH FOR HIM
BY PROTECTIVE ARTIST PAINTED IN.
AND THE LECHEROUS EYE DEVOURS
WITH DERISION FOR SIX WHOLE HOURS.
YET... IN HIS GRACE HE CRIED,
"FATHER, FORGIVE."
WHY, GOD?

13. "WHY?" WE ALL CRY,
"DO WE SUFFER AND DIE?"
HOW COULD A GOD OF LOVE
STAND AND STARE
AT THE SENSELESS AGONIES
WE SHARE?
WHY US?

14. SEE THAT MAN ON THE TREE?
HE UNDERSTANDS YOUR PAIN.
HE WAS TEMPTED LIKE YOU AND ME,
AND HE WILL COME AGAIN,
FOR THOSE WHO BELIEVE IN HIS NAME,
TO BRING VICTORY.
HOW COULD HE BEAR TO SHARE
IN OUR SUFFERING?
THE ONLY ANSWER IS:
LOVE.
THAT'S BECAUSE HE'S GOD.

The God Who Washes Feet

A Poem

1. What do you expect the gods to do?
How should they behave?
Would they take much notice of you?
Or sit on their throne
Alone
And issue commands
And make you slave?
Or use their authority
And superiority
To cause your inferiority?
Whatever they do
It will prove who
Has the right
To rule with might.

2. BUT WITH OUR GOD
IT'S A DIFFERENT STORY.
HE LEFT HIS PLACE OF GLORY,
LAID ASIDE HIS MAJESTY
VOLUNTARILY.
ACCEPTED HIS NATIVITY,
PREFERRED TO TAKE IDENTITY
WITH MAN IN HIS WORLD.

3. BEFORE THE SUPPER
IN THE UPPER ROOM
HIS DISCIPLES' DEBATE
DISCUSSED
WHO WOULD BE GREAT
IN THE KINGDOM,
AND THUS,
SIT IN STATE
NEXT TO THE KING
ON HIS RIGHT OR LEFT
AND BE MOST BLESSED.

4. SO AFTER SUPPER
IN THE UPPER ROOM,
THE GOD OF CREATION
CHOSE
TO SET ASIDE HIS CLOTHES.
OUR LORD
POURED

WATER IN A BASIN
AS A DECLARATION
OF HIS SERVANTHOOD
THAT HE EMBRACED.
HE TOOK A TOWEL
AND PLACED
IT ROUND HIS WAIST
AND WASHED THE FOUL
SMELL OF THE STREET
FROM HIS DISCIPLES' FEET.

5.THIS PARABOLIC LESSON
WAS AN EXPRESSION
OF HIS SERVANT HEART,
THAT FROM THE START
HE SOUGHT
TO TEACH
EACH
OF US WE OUGHT
TO FOLLOW HIS EXAMPLE,
TO BRING BLESSING,
NOT TRAMPLE
ON THE DIGNITY OF OTHERS.
AND IF WE ASPIRE TO THE ELITE,
WE DO IT
BY WASHING
EACH OTHER'S FEET.

6. WHAT DO WE EXPECT THE GODS TO DO
TO EXPRESS THEIR RULE?
LAUD IT OVER OTHERS?
OUR GOD TREATED US
AS BROTHERS.
HE TOOK A TOWEL
AND WASHED THE FOUL
SMELL OF THE STREET
FROM OUR FEET.

Biblical reference: John 13:1–15

Acknowledgements

THERE ARE SEVERAL people in my life who have helped make this book possible.

First, I would like to thank my husband, David, who has encouraged me from the beginning and put up with me disappearing for hours in order to write it, as well as sitting patiently to listen whilst I have tried the stories out on him.

Also, I am extremely grateful to my youngest daughter, Charlotte, who, with her superior computer skills, helped me assemble the book into one document and correct my typing errors, despite the fact that she was studying for a qualification at the same time.

My other daughter and her family gave up an evening to help me decide on titles for the stories. And my granddaughter, Cara, read through some of the stories with the critical eye of a twelve-year-old, in the process of learning punctuation.

Finally, I am grateful to my Bible study group, who was willing to listen to me read some of the stories to them.

Ingram Content Group UK Ltd.
Milton Keynes UK
UKHW022024190323
418794UK00011B/275